EXCERPTUS
Child of Nosferatu

YEVA-GENEVIEVE LAVLINSKI

EXCERPTUS
Child of Nosferatu

Written by

YEVA-GENEVIEVE LAVLINSKI

ISBN-13: 978-0578405117
ISBN-10: 0578405113

Book Cover Art by
Yeva-Genevieve Lavlinski & Paul Hamilton Molinsky
Photographs by Paul Hamilton Molinsky

Printed and bound in the United States of America
First printing October 2018

www.nobleheir.com

CONTENTS

YEVA-GENEVIEVE LAVLINSKI

DEDICATION

To my beloved brother
Anatoliy Grigoriyevich Garbuzenko

The hollow cooing of the Cuckoo bird is the most anxious sound to me, even when I cover my ears. In Eastern Europe, it signifies the end of someone's life. That frightful cooing predicted too many of my losses.

"Your beloved brother died from the hand of a witch, a possessed woman he knew. She killed him slowly to keep everything where she wanted," whispered a voice as I leaned over my brother's coffin to say my last goodbye.

I gazed around and saw many faces whispering in prayer and then I looked straight ahead. There at the end of the gathered mourners, a little girl stood silently, a little girl I knew. It was not possible for her to whisper in my ear, she was too far away and how could a child say or know such darkness? I kept staring at the child, and she stared back at me.

Some lives are easy, and God helped them be that way. Other lives, those whom we never forget, are full of struggle and worry for both them and for those of us who love them deeply.

My beautiful blue-eyed brother Anatoliy Grigoriyevich was a talented musician and singer and will be loved forever. With multiple difficult attempts at life, he could not conform to the framed rules of common society but was rather hounded by it. In a single moment, Anatoliy was taken away from our mother and our family to become an angel in heaven. Veiled in the free-spirited character of Jacob in this book, I portray the deep and sensitive soul that my brother was while hiding his pain behind silly jokes as he tried to fit into the ordinary.

My brother ended the path of his talent at the request of his marriage. With his passion halted, he stopped growing and became a small-time event player and then finally quit. For over two decades, he sequestered his love for music, which led him to regular jobs and ultimately, alcohol. Becoming nobody, he became a burden to those who prevented him from being himself.

During my study at law school, I was involved in theatre. One day the director, Mrs. Knyazeva, hatefully said to me, "Stop playing a role in your tiny home theatre!" At that time, I was angry at her disrespect toward my family, but looking back at many loses, including my father and brother, I realize they could have done so much more with their talent, yet they were bound to serve their small limited demands of duty, influenced by communal judgment. In a consequential necessity of growing up fast, I feel qualified to rephrase my instructor's seeming hatefulness into a defense of talent and quality ambition, "If you must perform, perform for the whole world."

The kindness of my brother Anatoliy may be described as sunshine at the seaside with a little gentle breeze of mischief. Gifted with a sincere smile, my brother could easily play most instruments and had the unique ability to sing unknown songs after hearing only a few notes. He was loved in the street by strangers, by the homeless, and by the educated of high society. He was a tenderly loving father to his son, Mikhail, and daughter, Irina. My brother was sensitive as a cloud hurt by thunder that let out its pain through raindrops.

My sorrow will never end. My guilt of not saving him is not excused by being so far away and will be carried as stone on my heart.

Yet, nothing can compare to the tormenting horror of grief that our mother Tamara is going through. Seeing mothers suffer makes my mind want to fall asleep and wake up in the past when we all; my mother Tamara, my father Grigoriy, my brother Anatoliy, sister Valentina and I, were sitting at the dining table happily making plans for the future and eating watermelon from our garden, while my lovely brother played the accordion.

EXCERPTUS – CHILD OF NOSFERATU

ACKNOWLEDGMENTS

Thank you to my father, Grigoriy Danilovich Garbuzenko, for my childhood fairy tales that made my imagination so vivid. Dearest father, my appreciation for your parental discipline and freedom that established dignity in me and gave me the chance to discover my true calling, literature and filmmaking.

Endless thanks to my mother, Tamara Frunze-Sologub. You gave true unconditional motherly love that helped me develop my deep human perception and sensitivity.

Thank you to my beloved brother, Anatoliy Garbuzenko, as inspiration for this book.

Thank you to my sister, Valentina Garbuzenko, for taking care of everyday life, allowing me to pursue my dreams.

My sincere gratitude to my best friend ever, Paul Hamilton Molinsky, for all of your encouragement and support and untold hours of work on my projects. Your friendship is invaluable, your kindness is priceless.

Special thanks to David Glover for editing and reading the numerous drafts of this book. Thank you for being my mentor in English.

Thank you to my friend, Valentin Molodezkiy, who constantly insisted on developing my talents and demanded to exhibit my art.

EXCERPTUS – CHILD OF NOSFERATU

YEVA-GENEVIEVE LAVLINSKI

EXCERPTUS
Child of Nosferatu

CHAPTER 1

ARROGANCE OF YOUTH

CALIFORNIA, UNITED STATES - SUMMER

Gently caressed by the wind, a frail tail of a white headscarf seemed to be suggesting an escape from its attachment to the temple of a human head. This white flicker of silk in the lonely breeze revealed glimpses of Pacific blue and the bleached wooden deck of the anchored white yacht.

Fleeing the yacht and the human head was a naive intention, as beyond was an eternal field of water drops, the crossing of which could only be accomplished by a very experienced swimmer. This utopia of escape had been planted and harvested by the human mind of that very temple of attachment.

A mature female's voice slithered forth through the air, "It simply means that the realization of everything that each of us had so dearly planned may have been prevented by others in advance. What would be the meaning of such an act, you ask? Unlimited reasons. For one, it is to keep you where you are. The second is envy. The third is the fear of losing you and so on. But in the end, it comes down to its fundamental state: to keep you where you are."

The seductive female lips, prudently masking their aging state behind the wealth of an elegant Bacharach crystal flute, were reciting in between sips of champagne, "As we live, as we search, as we pause to digest our achievements in a moment of tiredness, we wish for serenity. We wish for long-term calmness, impossible to reach, alike the steadiness of water."

Seemingly contradicting the pronounced context, the ocean held its breath in a motionless lapse.

Her trembling lips, overflowing with held back desire, continued, "In this modern life, haste producing disagreements aim toward exhausting hate. However, objectively analyzing history, no body of water was ever still as no life was ever tranquil."

Framed by boyish cheeks and a red-lipped smile, the unrestrained blue eyes of the enchantingly handsome young Jacob agreed in their calm squinted manner. To stretch his naturally athletic nude torso, he stood up and reflexively grasped his loose white linen trousers that were falling below his hips. He gifted the atmosphere with a smile, once again.

The aged eyes of the female across from Jacob joyfully admired his bare visage and the linen covered elevation of his manhood. An untimely intrusion of the wind-driven scarf rudely interrupted her view. Reticently, she pushed her scarf away with her well-taken care of yet inevitably aging hands. She took another long look over her tilted glass allowing her mind to scream, "God All Mighty! Every inch of his body, every tiniest cell, is projecting youth. What would I do to be there again? How I would cherish my youth! How I would prize it!"

The natural curls of his hair brushed his bare shoulder as Jacob cavalierly spoke, "I'm hungry! Water makes me hungry."

"In a moment," the female replied in her delicate voice then rang a silver bell three times; the sound was almost drowned out by the ringing of her plethora of platinum bracelets.

Resembling the movement of a Middle Eastern prayer her thin-skinned hands slid down from her forehead to her chin, revealing a face that mourned for youth. Liz Wartz looked sixty, not overweight; not anemic; she just looked sixty. Select areas of her face were tight and unmoving from numerous plastic surgeries; other areas were tired and wrinkled. She could not go back and undo what she had done to her face in frustration, as she tried to pause the aging process in the last grasp of recapturing her youth. It was all so obviously visible, the reconstruction of her face as well as her regret of it. Liz was almost sure that Jacob saw her struggle so, she held onto her slipping confidence as tight as she could, and pondered the words of an old friend, "You must learn to love yourself as you are; otherwise, there is no meaning for this exhausting battle to prolong human life with our individual perception of vibrant living."

Dressed in a long white silk robe with a pleat at the bottom, that was beautifully waving over her gemstone-covered flats, Liz Wartz whispered, "What do you think of the writings?" Hoping for the disruption of the air to necessitate the shortening of their proximity to each other she gazed at Jacob.

"What writings?" Jacob replied with a scrunched up face to avoid the penetrating shine from Liz's enormous diamond earrings.

"Even your hearing is like a young hawk," she said with sarcasm. "The writing I have just read."

"Ah that," he smiled again. "It's very philosophical, but what do you, Miss Liz, know about tiredness and those sort of things? Looks like, even your fruit has been washed by servants."

"And what do you know about philosophical meanings?" she answered with a taint of arrogance, slipping out of her usual visage of self-control.

"I don't know much, but my philosophy is to live as before rules existed. Do what I want and feel what I want. That much I know."

"To have any kind of philosophical reasoning, a person must have a social experience. But I guess it is irrelevant to you my dear, as you don't place yourself within the borders of a social framework? Do you Jacob?"

"Nah," Jacob's word echoed his untidy attitude.

"In that case, in your world, other people can also do what they want," she paused, "To you."

Jacob's nonchalant gaze to the ocean projected the impression of barely thinking.

"Well let's eat. Besides, this conversation is most likely immaterial for the purpose of this trip," she said, while tactically controlling her range of emotions.

Thankfully, due to a precise lunch schedule, her butler's entrance interrupted their elongated silence.

With dark circles around his eyes, the butler of unknown ethnicity entered from below deck. He set down a tray of exquisite food, saving the deteriorating situation, "Lunch is served, My Lady."

"Sit, Jacob, eat and do what you do best, spread pleasure with your joyous smile," Liz said.

Relaxed and apparently ready to feast, Jacob replied in his easy-going way, "That I can definitely do."

"Your eyes naturally acclimatize to the exotic and spectacular, satisfying the surroundings while indulging themselves," Liz said with enormous favoritism but then realized that she just pronounced her thoughts out loud. Feeling like a thief caught at the crime scene, she quickly turned her interest to the meal.

Unusual for Jacob to read any predicament, he did, and semi-victoriously smiled at Liz.

After a few silent mouthfuls, Liz searched for any tells of thought on Jacob's face, but they were hidden well, or even worse, they were absent. The quiet pause was taking too long. For resolution, Liz interjected into the awkward moment so she could enjoy her meal, "Well, what I read was from one of the fabulous books of my old friend Knyazhna Zoryana. It is very true to a woman's nature."

"Kn-what-na? Is it like 'Tsar' and 'Tsarina' or something from Russian Royalty?"

"Well done, Jacob!" Liz exclaimed and finally lightened up. "Knyazhna Zoryana comes from Eastern European royal blood and, I believe, still treasures her noble title. She is an extraordinary lady and an exquisite writer. Though I don't like this word 'extraordinary' because it contains 'ordinary'; and ordinary is not something you use to describe the power of Knyazhna."

"Cool," Jacob murmured indifferently, while he

gulped down an oyster and loudly slurped his wine.

"I always..." started Liz.

"Is she...?" Jacob cut her off.

They laughed as they interrupted each other. Liz was delighted that they finally started a conversation with comfortable excitement. For a change, she saw a joyful sparkle of connection in Jacob's eyes, not simply a self-pleasing shine.

"Go on Jacob," Liz encouraged as she seductively placed a grape into her age-defining, slightly wrinkled mouth.

"I was just wondering if she lives in one of those medieval castles?" he asked as he sipped his wine and dropped a few pieces of cheese inside his mouth.

Liz stared at him with adoration, "Fun. I see you are genuinely asking a question and indeed wish to hear the answer. In fact, she does. Knyazhna has more than one castle from different architectural periods and with different interior designs. All, of course, have superb taste and comfort. At the moment she resides in one far away from any public settlement."

"Huh. Cool. I would love to visit a castle like that one day," replied Jacob with his limited vocabulary.

"Well, I am the perfect person to make that happen, a matchmaker for those wishes," Liz said lustrously as she drank her wine.

"That would be cool," reiterated Jacob and grabbed a chunk of grilled duck. With the meat in his mouth, he bent over, rolled up his light trousers then laid down on the deck of the yacht and chowed down on the bird.

With all her mind, Liz caressed Jacob's young tight skin, "Her castle is in a reclusive territory."

"Reclusive, what's that?" Jacob asked still chewing and carelessly gazing up at the sky.

"Far away from everyone," answered Liz.

"I love reclusive. I am tired of the overcrowding-noise and demands of this town," said Jacob, spreading his arms in enjoyment of his sunbath.

"It might not be so sunny there," she added.

"Fine. I am going to have fun inside a castle," Jacob imagined for a moment, "To be taken care of by servants and all that." He paused then laughed, "I am just joking. Servants."

"Do you think an elder Lady with all her means will be cleaning and cooking for herself? Of course she has help; she can afford dozens of servants," Liz Wartz answered as if her own pride of wealth was offended. Before her uncontrollable emotions became unpredictable, Liz caught herself trying to join her eyebrows in anger, which she knew was impossible from all the Botox injected overdose.

"I am sure she has assistants. Calm down Liz," Jacob said in his same relaxed tone and grabbed another piece of meat.

"Would you care for coffee, ma'am?" the butler interjected. His sudden appearance surprised Jacob.

"Thank you, that would be superb," Liz replied with the remnants of anger still visible on her face.

"Nothing for me, my man. What's your name? I did not get it," Jacob asked him.

"Mmm, excuse me, ma'am," the butler mumbled as he poured coffee into Liz's cup. He set the coffee pot down and walked away.

"That's cool, no name. Ha, ha, ha," Jacob poorly imitated laughter.

"Stop it Jacob!" scolded Liz.

"Don't punish me! Don't punish me!" Jacob raised his hands up in mock surrender.

"Not yet," said Liz with a devious smile.

Perhaps their game of exchanged words and intentions was one-sided. As much as Liz thought about each of her phrases, Jacob simply spat out words as they came. Liz was not sure if she wanted to share the details of the seclusive castle and its residents with Jacob. Opportunity to enter that world had drilled and tempted her mind multiple times, yet herself, she was not ready to commit.

In her thought, Liz revisited and reevaluated Knyazhna's invitation to travel to her latest residence, "What exactly will I lose in obtaining this prospect? Will it influence my decision to disconnect from my past? Will I have to say goodbye to all I remember?" Liz observed the profoundly reduced expression of existence on Jacob's face. "I don't know if I envy him or I pity him, but I do know for sure that if this glorious chance comes to him, he will only gain because he has no true attachment to common reality."

"I can definitely see myself being kept inside the castle walls," Jacob announced. "And relishing in it."

"Great," she said. "Your pay will be more than generous. In a very little time, you'll earn more money than you can make in years in your struggling modeling career. So much money that you will be free to truly do what you wish every day and never have to worry about petty cash or another bill-paying job. It's like winning the lottery."

"I have never won a buck in anything, let alone the lottery. I tried a casino once and lost more than I could. So, how am I to believe in this luck?" Jacob asked disbelievingly.

"You must be a gambler at some point of your life. Making timely appropriate choices at propositions. As simple as A, B, C. Take the offer or not. You won't get a second chance," Liz repositioned herself and softened her intense speech, "Unless, of course, someone seriously desires you."

"Like your talent?" Jacob asked sarcastically, half-hiding his supposition.

Liz laughed, "That could be too, Jacob. But in your case, your talent is physical."

"Okay," He smiled shyly, "Liz, Liz, Liz..."

"Oh, come closer," Liz wiggled her index finger in front of her face, inviting him to come her way.

Submissively, Jacob sat down next to her.

"Listen, Jacob. I am a serious businesswoman. My time is worth a lot. And what I say is gold. I am not in the custom to waste a penny. I have all sorts of prospects right at my fingertips," she said as she caressed his ear, then kissed and licked his nude shoulder, "But everything has a price."

"I am aware of that Liz," he answered with confidence.

"Bravo," Liz whispered, swallowing as she stared at his young lips.

Jacob placed a glass of wine between them and drank from it as Liz held her breath. As he finished, he grabbed Liz with vigorous hands. She let herself be, for whatever he was going to do.

Her mind whirled with possibilities, "I don't care if he slaps my face or throws me overboard. I insanely crave the physical contact of his youth, must have it and will."

Jacob pushed Liz back while still holding her and then slid his hand under the silk covering her shoulder. He looked straight into her eyes, then pulled her back in and kissed her passionately.

In this tiniest fragment of her life, Liz was willing to part with most of her possessions in exchange for bewitching Jacob's soul.

Jacob suddenly released his grip on her, took a step back and asked, "What is it you want from me, Liz?"

"In exchange for your eternal financial freedom, I simply want to experience what my clients do," her eyes penetrated his, "From you."

"And what are they telling you they have experienced, Liz?" the question eased from Jacob's gentle smile.

Liz let out a slightly wavering breath, "Whatever it is that warrants the huge commission that I receive. It must be impressive."

"But they are clients, and you are my boss. What if I don't find it...?"

Liz interrupted Jacob, "Listen, without these clients and without my backing, you will end up working in fast food, burning your lovely skin in overcooked oil."

"You speak so knowledgeably about fast food as if you once worked there, Lizzy?"

"Hilarious joke, Jacob. However, your job is not to check on my past, but to keep me happy in the present and in the future."

"How happy, Liz?" questioned Jacob spreading his smile.

Liz looked at the front of his pants that was elevated with the strength of his youth. "Preferably..." she raised her eyes to meet his, "Very happy."

"Oh, yeah?" he smiled touching his groin. He picked out a cigar from the humidor near him, lit it and watched her through puffs of rising smoke. Liz sipped her now cold coffee. She set it down, grabbed a glass of champagne and drank it with gusto. Exposing her tanned legs, Liz stood up and walked over to Jacob, who took one more half-inhale of his cigar.

"Just a moment boss," Jacob threw away the cigar and stretched up looking directly at Liz. He slowly loosened his pants, dropped them exposing his nude sexuality to Liz's love-hungry eyes and jumped overboard.

Insulted, Liz knew that Jacob jumped not for a swim but to get away from her. "I'll keep that proposal until you crawl back to me," holding her face against the wind to calm herself she whispered, "I am not easily disappointed!" While leaning over the boat rail, Liz shouted down to the ocean, "Come back when you feel like it! Don't take long; everyone is substitutable in this town!"

Perfectly hearing her warning, Jacob joyfully swam away.

A touch of worry overcame Liz's rage, "It is too far to the shore." She looked at the calm water and reassured herself, "With his young body and free spirit he will make it."

"Ma'am," the butler without a name, raised up from his respectful bow, "Would you care for any other refreshment?"

At that moment a large seagull floating next to the yacht gave up on waiting for pity scraps and suddenly took off, splashing Liz's face. Knocked by a wave of reality she awoke from her desire. "That'll be all for now," she answered her awaiting butler who handed her a towel and walked away. Liz stared at the fearless body disappearing from her view, separated farther and farther by distance. She removed her silk headscarf and let it have its freedom it seemed to desire so. At first, the scarf blasted off like a racehorse out of the gates; then it glided in the air floating on the winds of freedom. In a flash, it fell in the endless ocean, which extinguished its short flight. Liz smirked, to feel joy over the fallen was her natural character. To her, it was victory. Making a bet to herself, she counted in her head how many days until this wild free-spirit would meet his debt-drowned end. "See you soon, Jacob. See you soon."

CHAPTER 2

LUCRATIVE ASSIGNMENT

EASTERN EUROPEAN FIELD - DAY
(ONE YEAR LATER)

The friendly, baby blue sky contributed to the general splendor of an early European Spring. The surrounding merriness of nature throughout the widespread land was assisted by a festive wind. The small locally manufactured half-century old rusted bus bumped along like a toy on the uneven Eastern European road. The greenery of the fields was a visual representation of true vital energy, with its refreshing abundant release of the chemical element atomic number 8, the life-supporting component of the air, oxygen.

The handsome face of a young man, unfit to be

among the bus's scratched windows, tiredly gave up on looking through the blurriness. Seemingly endless fields were leading their roads toward a reedy forest. Half a mile before a border of trees, the bus stopped, and a single passenger stepped off at this rare destination. The bus made a U-turn and drove away. The slickly-dressed man placed his suitcases on the ground then stood up to reveal his face. It was Jacob. He stretched his arms and legs and looked in front of him to the rising tree border, which beyond its reedy appearance, conveyed the impression of a terrestrial guardian projecting warnings.

Jacob believed that this weird unsafe feeling was simply the effect of his difficult travel, along with his inner conversation about the decision of taking on the trip, while already being on the road. "I must stop," he commanded himself. "Who would try to make the decision about going on the trip while being on the trip?" He lifted his leg for another stretch and noticed that his shoes were getting stuck in the muddy soil. "That's great, that's all I need," he exclaimed. The words repeated in his head like bells in a chapel belfry.

Jacob looked around for any prospects of comfort, locating nothing except the spread of grass implanted with islands of puddles like a muffin with raisins. His doubt of any possibility of civilized service confirmed itself as he peered through the border of random trees and saw further, a dense forest. "Field, mud, and impenetrable forest. Nice," Jacob described to himself. A squeaky sound raised his hopes for company. "Any company," he shouted and made an attempt to turn towards the noise, but only his head seemed to be willing to move. His feet were stuck, "Right, what else?" With a lot of effort, he pulled his shoes out of the wet slimy dirt and walked to the signpost, which was a board that hung from two rusty chains with a very crude drawing of a horse, "Better stay here or the 'intellectual' locals might pass me by." He returned for his luggage and dragged them to the supposed horse station.

What seemed a tranquil eternity, was in fact, a mere thirty minutes. "However, this is an adventure!" Jacob yelled with excitement as he snacked on a protein bar that he pulled out of his inner jacket pocket, his emergency reservoir.

His mind picked up where his voice left off, "What's so exciting about California! No seasonal weather, a harbor with boats, palm trees and the only clean streets are in Beverly Hills? It's all an illusory fib of those claiming to be open-minded. Here I am at the..." He looked around and noticed the changing weather, "At nowhere. Piss where you want to land, and no one..." He got up and shouted, "No one to judge you!" The possibility of freedom and future wealth tickled his feet. Jacob sat on his suitcase and moved his feet around like a kid going to an amusement park. He removed his socks and extended his legs parallel to the ground, trying to keep balance with his arms, but fell. Luckily he landed just near a slimy puddle. He laughed and rolled around on the grass.

"What about your suit, Sir Jacob?" he asked

himself. "I must not worry of such trivial things. I will soon have hundreds of suits." Then his face turned serious. "Not yet, Sir," Jacob objected to his own two-faced conversation, "Please do not discourage me, you miserable son of a beatch."

The sun began to retire and its rapid disappearance reflected Jacob's declining mood. He sat back on the suitcases and started to wonder if he should set up his tent as he was advised by someone whose name he did not recall. Jacob opened the suitcases and pulled out a small travel tent and assembly manual. Unfortunately understanding it, for him, was as difficult as reading a scientific book. With a lot of frowning and page bending on the top corners, he gave up on the instructions. Jacob tried to dial a number on his cell phone, but there was no signal. All he heard was a thin penetrating screech.

It took him a while to turn hysterical, "Oh God! Oh God! Oh God! Why did I agree? Oh God! I want to be on a yacht, I want to be on a jet. Ahhhhahhhhahhhh!" As he continued to whine, the sunset and light became darkness, which Jacob observed with horror. Acting as if he had the power to stop the darkness, he gestured wildly with his hands and screamed, "AHHHHHAAAA! Help! Anyone! Ahhhhh!" He threw off his jacket, kicked a suitcase open, grabbed a handful of protein bars and started stuffing his mouth. He washed them down with water until he was dizzy, then finally found the courage to say out-loud his suspicion of the event, "She did it intentionally because I rejected her. Did you plan to murder me, Liz?! Did you?! You old witch!"

Giving up on his powerless predicament, Jacob repositioned his two suitcases next to each other and lay down on top of them. Falling asleep he mumbled, "I felt it was inappropriate for me to have intimate relations with my boss!!!! I felt it was inappropriate." He nervously screamed, "Can you hear me? You..?" He rolled over and fell onto the ground as a disturbing memory of only two days earlier flashed in his mind.

PHOTO STUDIO, LOS ANGELES
(TWO DAYS AGO)

In front of a large canvas lit by an array of studio lights, Jacob, sensual poster boy model, posed with an air of indifference. His shoulder length hair and sweet smile exposed his sexuality in its laziness. Synched flashes from the camera repeatedly blinded Jacob. However, even his reflexive hand blocking of the light from his eyes visually suited him. The queer, short, confident photographer tried to cheer up his model, "Excellent! Imagine an astonishing, extraordinary life!"

The cell phone rang. Without any concern of interrupting the photoshoot, Jacob answered, "Jacob speaking. Who?" He paused in question, "I almost forgot the tone of your voice." Unfazed by the unprofessional behavior of his model, the photographer continued clicking away. For a few moments, the conversation over the phone was one-sided. Jacob leaned against the background canvas, then sat on the floor, then again stood up.

"Excellent, a business call!" exclaimed the photographer as he seemingly admired every callous movement of his fashionable subject, and enthusiastically continued the photoshoot.

"How much?" Jacob arrogantly asked into the phone.

"Yes! Making corporate decisions!" the photographer kept repositioning up and down left and right in an attempt to capture the perfect angle at the perfect moment.

Jacob pulled the phone away from his ear and covered it with his hand as he looked at the photographer, "I don't need to imagine anything, I make an astonishing living." Jacob pulled a few coins out of his pocket, "Keep your petty cash." He dropped coins on the floor and iced it with the five hundred dollars that the photographer just gave him. Jacob grabbed his designer carry-on bag and walked away, not looking back.

The corner of Wilshire Boulevard and Rodeo Drive shined with the golden California sun and seemed to breathe out joy, as it usually did any time of the year. Jacob felt that he was right where he belonged, the social heart of Beverly Hills. Even though the clock said 2 pm Pacific time, for Jacob it was still morning, so he looked around for a coffee shop. He walked past Rodeo Drive and approached the glass door of 10400 Wilshire. When he pulled on the entrance door, it was locked. He tried again harder. Still closed. He looked through the window; the whole floor was under construction.

"What a witch! Liz played me," Jacob turned his back to the glass door and kicked it. He dropped his bag, squatted down and started digging through it for his phone. He dialed Liz's number and as soon as a voice answered, he screamed, "What the...?! I dropped my first paying job in a year! You can gloat in your usual winning. Well played."

Jacob cut his words short as the door buzzed and clicked. He hurried through the door across the lobby and into the elevator. The elevator's walls were covered in gray construction blankets. Jacob felt uncomfortable alone inside an elevator which might not be fully functional. As soon as the doors opened, he ran out as if someone was chasing him. The corridor was empty, too. As he hurried down the hallway, he saw a familiar sign on the door: "INSPIRATION - AGENCY." Jacob walked straight in.

Over the reception desk hung a larger sign, "INSPIRATION ESCORT AGENCY". The door to the main office was wide open as if expecting someone, perhaps him.

"Long time no see, no hear Lizzy!" Jacob acted like nothing awkward had ever happened between them. He stopped at the antique table adorned by a small gold plaque with the engraved words, Liz Wartz - Owner.

Wearing large dark sunglasses, Liz moved her long gray hair over her newly augmented, slightly exposed breasts, "Here," she pushed an agreement across the desk toward Jacob.

"Still looking dazzling, Miss Wartz," Jacob dropped his rear onto the chair across from her. He lied, as no new bust could hide Liz's merciless over sixty aging state.

"Read, make a quick decision, then either sign or don't," Liz proposed with indifference.

"Why me? A few bit parts, B-list at best. I'm only a slim, sensual actor banished from the presence of your wealthy society. What is the need of me now?" Jacob positioned himself in the chair like posing for a portrait.

Caring less for Jacob's behavior, Liz relied, "Your previous improvisation overwhelmed most of my clients."

"You once enjoyed being overwhelmed by me? Or, to be exact, wished to be..."

Liz's look interrupted him, "All I am interested in is making money. I have a request from a client yearning for an improvisation of love, for a free-spirited cupid, for someone just like you. In fact, no one else plays the part as well as you do. Eat, drink, be caressed a few times, be spoiled and get paid well." She pointed to the contract. "Your last chance to fix your financial situation and improve your social status. My little 'Love Spread.' Read all that is marked."

"Yeah, I am good at it," he pointed at himself with two fingers and ran them down his body to the end of his zipper. Jacob mumbled through the agreement briefly and moved on to the description. "An extraordinary, temperamental mature writer requires a young free-spirited, 'cupid looking' male to perform a muse duty, who is not limited by being pampered, as inspiration for her novel. Distant travel and possible discomfort will be greatly compensated. Bla, bla, bla, bla, bla," Jacob said then quickly signed. "Fine. Love it. Thanks. What now?"

Without speaking, Liz pulled the document away and placed the plane ticket and a stack of cash on the table, "You leave in two hours. The rest of the down payment will be in your account in twenty minutes."

"Sweet. Why so much cash?" Jacob's lips were inflamed with a healthy redness, as might a young girl's when she received her first expensive present from a wealthy older admirer.

Liz answered quickly, as if to nullify any concerns, "There will be no credit cards, nor habituated transportation where you are going. You will be traveling by carriage over a land called 'Lybid', to her isolated castle."

"I already love the name," Jacob interrupted. "Sounds like libido. However, social factors, such as work and relationship issues," Jacob pointed at Liz, "And internal psychological factors, such as my sensitive personality, can affect my libido. I took the time to learn how to handle my biological factors in my lifestyle, such as hormones, primarily testosterone, to keep my sex drive healthy. So getting out of LA will be very organic."

Liz could not believe that this was Jacob speaking; he seemed ready to accommodate many needs. She almost sensed the obedience, but she had seen that before. Once young people are out of money for a while, they lose their arrogance because of the need to pay for the path to their dreams. And in Los Angeles, every other person, young or old is a dreamer.

"May I finish?" asked Liz.

"Need help?" smiled Jacob, teasing her.

Liz ignored Jacob's remarks. She knew him too well and thought, "That free-spirited son of a Cuckoo might change his mind any time." Then she spoke, "In Slavic languages, 'Lybid' means swan, the symbol of grace and devotion. It is said that a swan is silent throughout all of its life, yet before its death, or if a swan looses its partner, it may choose to die. Then, at the last moment of life, a single magnificent metaphorical performance is given, when the swan sings as no other bird can sing." She spoke looking out the window and then turned back to make sure that Jacob was still there. And there he was, picking jelly beans from Liz's crystal vase tossing them up into his mouth. "There is also the Lybid River that runs through the city of Kiev," Liz carried on. "Its name comes from a legend that the three founders of Kiev had a sister, Lybid. Escaping invaders, Lybid found a safe land. In order to protect her wounded beloved, she transformed herself into a white swan and dropped her ghostly feathers, turning them into fog, preventing outsiders from finding their seclusive paradise."

"How's that legend supposed to be important to me?" Jacob asked with zero concern.

"That supposedly happened in the land you are going to," she answered.

"Right. Lybid, libido, see the connection?" facetiously remarked Jacob.

Liz was not sure if he was trying hard to be her favorite again or if he was trying to make her hate him, so she would not attempt again to gain possession of his physique; his soul had no interest to her. Liz sensed he was playing some nutty game. Not amused nor wanting to prolong the conversation, Liz Wartz answered dryly, "It is mostly flat land, invaded by constant fog, which makes the castle appear as if it is in the clouds. Tourists do not attempt to get there, due to fear of becoming lost. But you are expected there and will be guided." She looked at Jacob with apparent indifference and saw a hint of hesitation, so she smiled, "It is a very enchanting place. As an artistic person, you will be taken with it or by it."

"Fog, clouds, swans or cows, it's all fine with me. A carriage is cool, too! Tired of yachts, and jets, and small dogs!" And then he heard an angry yap of a tiny dog coming from under the table. "That little rat was hiding there all this time?" asked Jacob, then shut his mouth and openly laughed into his hand.

Liz threw a glass of water in his face and gestured for him to get out, "Bon voyage." The little dog was still yapping.

"Oh, water!" Jacob grabbed everything she had given him and blew her a sweet kiss, "You still can't get over our last voyage?" Characteristically to his nature, Jacob left as a free man. Full of optimism and excitement to get away from LA, he joyfully sang, "Hit the trippy road, Jacob! Hit the road boom, Jacob!"

Liz's eagerness for her intricate revenge was disguised behind her artificially stretched power smile. She kept that look fixated on Jacob's departing performance until he turned the corner; leaving her sight for good.

EASTERN EUROPEAN FIELD - EVENING

Covered by drops of evening dew, the upper surface of Jacob's body and face was now recognizable only by its silhouette; the rest was seemingly devoured by the darkness of the European field. While he lay there on the ground half aware of his own situation, time was passing slowly. A weird sound bothered his ear, "Phr PRGGR." Jacob opened his eyes and saw large nostrils that were breathing hot steam into his face. The heavy breathing fogged his view, which Jacob did not mind. Rather than feeling relieved to be found, he was delirious from the cold ground that zapped the heat from his body. He had no desire to face the reality of the circumstance, and he slowed his breath trying to put himself back to sleep. The technique to fight insomnia that he once heard from a stranger who claimed to be a yoga instructor, wasn't successful, but at least Jacob distracted himself by recalling the event and place of how they had met, which also eluded him.

A man without any specific visual distinction of appearance bent forward, picked Jacob up and assisted him onto the one horse open wagon. The man did not try to see if Jacob was dead or alive. He did not seem to care. Half-awake, Jacob felt the warmth of a patterned rug on top of the hay in the flat back of the wagon. He thought that it could have been an Oriental rug he had seen in windows of small boutique shops in LA. The smell of fresh hay tickled his nostrils. He was not sure how he could have known this aroma, but it made him feel safe. It was strange that he began to associate touch and smell like never before, contrary to his recent life from a few days ago.

Jacob first opened his eyes to a dark sky and then found the back of the man in charge of the wagon.

Comforted by the 'Perrggh' of the horse, Jacob placed his hand on the man's back, "Excuse me. Do you speak English?"

Continuing to guide the horse, the man gently pushed Jacob's hand away, then turned and looked at him with no sign of understanding. Jacob lay down and peacefully observed the sky. During the rest of the travel in the carriage, he was content to think of nothing. Soon, his eyes and mind started falling into a deep sleep.

CHAPTER 3

WELCOME TO THE RECLUSIVE CASTLE

EUROPEAN CASTLE, COURTYARD – NIGHT

Through his dream, Jacob felt his body collide with the objects around him when the wagon suddenly stopped. A resounding heavy metallic noise that must have awoken most of the neighboring farmland, spurred the horse forward. When Jacob's eyes reopened to a sliver, he saw a massive tarnished gate, loudly closing behind them. He slightly lifted his head and found himself in a country courtyard, guarded by unrefined stone walls. A little to the left, he dimly identified a centuries-old sophisticated grand building which external walls were unrefined as well.

"What is this place? I must have fallen asleep," Jacob asked his faceless guide. The man mumbled something that Jacob was not able to comprehend.

"That must be the hotel?" Jacob asked rhetorically. Again, the man did not seem to follow the question. He took Jacob's suitcases and walked in the direction of the grand unrefined building.

"Or is this the castle of my assignment, my final destination?" re-inquired Jacob louder, hoping for a response from his guide who had already dissipated into the darkness behind the enormous door of the vast building.

Stepping down from the wagon Jacob looked around and yelled, "Hello? Anyone else?" Then he explained to himself, "It must be the castle." Then yelled again, "Hello! Anyone!"

From a distance, the howling of wolves wafted over the gigantic stone walls. Startled, Jacob turned around, and to his bewilderment, there was no horse, no wagon, no one at all. Adding to his distress, a massive winged bird, producing a most unpleasant hissing, flew over his head. While momentarily ducking, the corner of Jacob's darting vision caught a bit of cozy light, which suddenly became an open door for his supposed welcome to the supposed castle.

"Castle it is," Jacob confirmed to himself.

The castle looked down on him with gothic arched windows, as the light from the night sky exposed their black emptiness. Jacob looked harder and spotted a change in that unfriendly hollowness; the shapes of figures in hooded robes were now evident at each and every window, as if studying the newcomer. Doubting his tired vision, Jacob told himself, it was the play of the night lights. A sudden swift wind whisked by Jacob toward the onlooking grand building of the castle, moving the door slightly more ajar.

"A sign to walk in?" Not accustomed to questioning an open door, Jacob wondered, "What other choice do I have? The carriage is gone. Even if there are creepy ghosts, I'm sure, inside the castle is safer then here in this courtyard." The immense, gigantic gate slammed hard behind him, adding confirmation to his conclusion. Not eager to look back, Jacob noticed a shadowy reflection on the ground of an enormous figure coming towards him from behind. Thunder rattled vibrating Jacob's nerve. He ran.

EUROPEAN CASTLE, CORRIDOR – NIGHT

Jacob rushed up the grand building's stairway and stopped. Overcoming his tugging fear he finally harnessed his adventurous spirit and crossed the steel frame of the castle's inviting vacancy. The thick wooden door closed sharply behind him, blowing out the candles' fragile flames.

Standing in complete darkness, he recollected in remarkable detail the external entrance guarded by the metal portcullis with its arrow tipped ends. Centuries ago, this type of iron gate would have been lowered to block access, to protect the main keep of the castle from intruders. Jacob was wondering if it came down, would it ever be able to be raised again. At that moment, he heard the crashing fall of the rusty portcullis seal the entry closed.

Beyond the thick wood of the great door, he could hear the sound of the coming storm. Jacob took a few more steps and proceeded forward into the inner blackness. A prolonged exhale behind him caused his heart to skip a beat. He quickly turned around, "Hah! Excuse me."

A small, dark, hooded figure spoke with a tired whispery voice, "I am glad to welcome you into the main keep of the castle. The journey was difficult and unusual for you. Please follow me."

"Hello. You said where? Main, what, keep? Castle right?" Jacob tried to process the welcome observing the bizarre host and thought, "At least it's small, whoever it is." He then asked, "Excuse me, is that a question?" Jacob blindly followed the little figure trying to figure out if it was bending or perhaps crooked. The hooded figure did not answer but continued to lead, seemingly moving like a puppet floating on strings, or on a single based suspension pole. Under the gliding fabric of the long dress, Jacob could not observe any steps being made by the host's feet. Additionally, he was intensely determined to find out the color of the figure's outfit. "Was it black, brown or dark green?" he pondered while he had no idea why it was important for him at that moment. Jacob opened his eyes as wide as he could to the point of pain. He screamed in his mind, "Awwee! That hurts, I hope I did not damage my eyeballs."

"No," anemically answered the dark figure.

Jacob swallowed. "How the hell did the sliding figure know my thoughts?" he thought.

"My statement was a reply about your question about your unusual travel," the dark figure whispered weakly.

"Yes, it was unusual, and thank you," Jacob continued to try to see through the darkness. In his mind he engaged himself in a frivolous self-conversation to camouflage his deductions and suppositions, "I wonder if this is one of the servants that Liz mentioned? She did not mention anyone in particular. She said there must be servants. Oh well, this is already overwhelming. I am so ready, even dreadfully impatient in my expectation, to be pampered as a muse should be."

EUROPEAN CASTLE, LIVING ROOM – NIGHT

As Jacob and the small hooded figure exited the blackness of the corridor, they walked into a living room barely lit by candles. By the shape and the way the guiding figure was softly moving, Jacob judged it was an elderly woman with a hump, "She is a clearly a hunchback. A maid perhaps." Because of her petite body and the way she was bending, the hump looked larger than it was. Still not being able to see her face, he shrugged and continued to tail after the little-crooked lady.

Something about the way she walked bothered him. He did not understand if she was weak, her feet were hurting or maybe she was riding a wireless remote control electric skate board. He redirected his attention again toward her feet but was unable to detect anything underneath her excessively dragging dress. "The poor hunchback thing is also probably crippled," Jacob made another observatory conclusion and almost bumped into her when the hooded petite suddenly stopped.

Jacob quickly stepped back and raised his inquisition-like gaze from her feet, as if it never happen. He finally noticed that they had arrived at a strangely decorated, spacious hall. Nothing matched one distinct style. This disturbed Jacob and at the same time amused him. He recalled one of his affairs as an escort with an older Portuguese lady, a millionaire. She told him a story about a pearl of a very irregular shape that was named Barocco. That pearl, she claimed, gave rise and namesake to the style of the Baroque period, which she somehow associated with Jacob's appearance. Jacob felt the same about this place. It was erratic in its design as well as exquisite. One side of the room was highly ornate and extravagant, yet the wall behind the table clashed against it with unfinished medieval roughness.

When they reached a vast table, the hooded petite lady stopped and offered, "Please take this chair." Without question, Jacob sat down. As the hooded petite walked away, Jacob studied the table. It had wonderful elaborate and elegant wood work dating back to the time of the Renaissance. Because of its massiveness, the table must have never been moved. With enormous portions of meat, whole loaves of bread, large silverware and platters, the feast, could have served an either a medieval wedding or party, yet was only set for two. Jacob swallowed, trying not to break any European traditions unknown to him. He waited patiently, staring around and admiring the chandeliers with their candles. Then he saw his hooded guide again, she talked to someone tall in the dim corner. Soon the hooded old lady dissolved into the tall figure's shadow and disappeared completely out of sight. Merging with candle light, the towering man carrying a silver bowl inserted himself into the visible part of the living room. Setting the bowl on the table in front of their guest Jacob, the towering man slightly smiled with his surprisingly rosy-cheeks. Jacob was pleased to finally meet a normally appearing man, "Hello! What is it?" he said and looked inside the bowl.

"Good evening, Sir. To wash your hands," answered tall, accommodating man. He held a long pause while studying Jacob.

"Yes! Good evening!" Jacob happily exclaimed and promptly rolled up his sleeves and began to wash his hands with joy, "What is your name?"

"My name is Bohdan. I serve in this house," the impressive man of height and posture replied as he handed a towel to Jacob, who was captivated with the unfamiliar situation.

Bohdan patiently waited for Jacob to splash his face. He then poured water from a silver pitcher for a rinse, collected the towel, bowl and was about to walk away when their guest spoke, "I am Jacob, the Inspirer, the Muse, from LA. It's Los Angeles, United States, you know, America?" Not seeing any recognition of his words on the servant's face Jacob asked, "When do I meet Mrs. Knyazhna ahh something Z...?"

"It is known to us who you are. Sir. No one comes here uninvited," said Bohdan, holding his servant's posture.

"Sure," Jacob stated impertinently.

Bohdan lifted his eyebrows.

"Certainly," Jacob corrected himself and gestured to Bohdan to continue. "Please go on."

For a moment, Bohdan stared at the guest, then began to march a few steps on the same spot as if he was practicing military drills. After the shock subsided, Bohdan added, "And there is definitely no trespassing. Her Majesty Knyazhna Zoryana will join you shortly. Please start alone." The servant's words cut off sharply as he walked away toward the entrance door.

Not impressed a bit with the title of his new employer, Jacob replied, "Majesty totally works for me." He hungrily started eating without even putting food on his plate. After a few brief moments, Jacob saw Bohdan pass by on the second floor balcony. As Jacob was filling himself with a tasty serving, he observed the old crooked petite, who had welcomed him earlier in her hooded coat, appear from the dim corridor leading to what he supposed was the kitchen. She began to wash her hands in a very meticulous way in a large ornate metal bowl. While rinsing her hands the crooked petit whispered to a tall dark figure. She never once glimpsed toward Jacob, who pondered, "I wonder who she is? A nanny? A house keeper? I don't know. Who cares. I'll find out soon enough."

As Jacob watched the old lady's routine of cleanliness, he was full of curiosity as he tried to recognize who the faceless, tall figure near her was, "It can't be that big Bohdan, I just saw him walking upstairs." Jacob started to doubt himself. The more he observed the tall figure, the more he was sure it was Bohdan, but it was impossible to identify anyone for certain in such darkness.

Drinking excessively to wash the food down, Jacob let his eyes wander around the room. While swallowing a chunk of meat he almost choked, becoming fully present in the moment.

A few moments passed and Bohdan walked in slowly, supporting the right arm of the familiar, hooded hunchback-petite lady. Jacob could now finally catch the deep emerald green color of her dress shifting to a brown black and back, depending on the light. Bohdan being at the same time in different places, confused Jacob, but his mind justified it with all kinds of possibilities, like fast ways to get from one place to another, perhaps on elevator, or maybe Jacob was mistaken in seeing Bohdan in two places at once. As Bohdan was helping the emerald hooded lady to be seated at the other side of the table, she pushed him away, as old people often do, to deny their age-limiting dependency.

"Geeez!" exclaimed Jacob in his mind, "The crookedness, the hump, the faceless hood. Could this be my new boss?!"

Fascinated by Jacob's facial expression, the old hooded lady scuffled her feet under the table.

Jacob leaned over staring with the excitement at the exposed sliding slippers of the hooded lady, that her robe had hidden before. The shape of her curled toe shoes reminded him of a Venetian gondola. Jacob described the shoes in his mind, "Looks like that boat for traveling canals like we travel streets, the Italian one, the gondola. Or even more like Jester sandals." Amused, Jacob studied her shoes that were covered in shiny stones and their tips were excessively curved up and over.

Observing the quality of her footwear made Jacob give up on his first thought that the old hunchback could have been a maid or a servant.

"Are you by chance a Knya-zhna?" he asked her while trying to see her face shaded by her hood. A blinding candle right in front of him and none at her side of the table, made it virtually impossible for him to recognize anything at all.

"May I introduce, Her Majesty Knyazhna Zoryana," announced Bohdan, straightening his body in pride.

Knyazhna noticed Jacob's interest was directed toward her footwear rather than her title, so she bragged about her exquisite shoes as any young lady might do, "These are antique traditional Turkish upturned slippers. They first appeared in Anatolia around 1600 BC."

"Cool flip-flops!" Jacob exclaimed then held off momentarily to figure out what to say next, "Knyaz-hna! Okay then, Knyazhna. Can I call you Mrs. or Miss? That is how we refer to a woman in America."

"You may call me Knyazhna Zoryana, as I was called in my early years," aristocratically handling the situation, Knyazhna interrupted Jacob's contemporary frank rudeness.

"Your Majesty?" Bohdan began to whisper but was stopped by the powerful hand of the hooded

Knyazhna.

"Ladyship will do," said Knyazhna to Bohdan. "Or we will confuse and scare the boy."

"As you wish, Your Ladyship," bowed Bohdan.

Jacob blinked, "I would love to know about your title. So are you like noble royalty?"

"There is a big difference," Knyazhna irritatingly answered. She raised her skinny finger to give Bohdan permission to speak.

"Royalty is an inherited title," Bohdan began, "Where as nobility can be earned for political, military or financial achievements, yet it does not exclude royal blood. The historical Slavic title, 'Knyaz' was used as both a royal and noble title in different times of history. It originated in the times of Kievan Russ, from Knyazhna Zoryana's predecessor, Knyaz Ivan. In 1500 Knyaz Ivan was crowned as Tzar, which means King. In your English, Knyaz is translated as Prince, Duke or Count,"

"However, there is clearly an un-clarity in the purity of royal blood," added Knyazhna.

"We don't practice that kind of royal stuff in America. Of course, children inherit money or property but not like titles," Jacob shared his knowledge. Bohdan repeated his unrelated marching in the same spot. Jacob took it as a clue to change the topic, "I would imagine the European rules for guests of the house are different than in America?"

"Please. Don't bring your rules into a house that you are guest in, especially this house, Sir," Bohdan stopped marching and interjected in a sharp tone.

"Got'ya," Jacob affirmed in urban American slang, then added, "I will try my best."

"Pardon me," Bohdan excused himself and once again dissolved into the kitchen corridor as if sucked into a dark tunnel at night.

To say a proper hello, Jacob got up and walked to Knyazhna Zoryana. As he reached her, he stopped as if hit by a shockwave, seeing for the first time inside the hood, the woman of a very great age, perhaps over one hundred years old. Her extremely dehydrated pale skin hung over her Eastern European skull without any appearance of muscle, and there was no sign of hair.

Jacob felt uncomfortable being shocked at her appearance and hoped she did not notice his reaction. "I know I am not that horrible of a person but who could expect this?" he thought then stopped with an overwhelming feeling of fear that someone could hear the thoughts in his mind. It was the same sensation he obtained when he first entered the residence crossing the great castle gate. The sensation, misleading Jacob's perception of actuality, appeared whenever he was thinking, confusing his thought with mumbling, that might be heard by others. "Mrs. Knya-zh-na Zo-rya-na. Allow me to express my appreciation for my honorable position," unable to complete the virtue of his compliment Jacob extended his hand.

The well-mannered Knyazhna appeared to sympathize with Jacob's attempt in phrasing flattery, yet she sternly directed, "You must wash your hands before offering it to a Lady." The words that left her mouth also left it slightly open, her jaw had fallen down, which was natural for old bones and gravity.

"Right," said Jacob, wiping his hand on his pants. The awkwardness of the moment was distracted by Bohdan, who brought an elaborate five-stemmed silver candelabra and placed it in front of Knyazhna Zoryana. The flickering clarifier even more so deteriorated the facade of old Knyazhna's lifeless face. It stunned Jacob to his core, which made him improve his manners, "Sure, pardon me. Your Majesty." But instead of leaving he remained in the same spot.

An unexpected whiff slid Knyazhna's hood back and revealed a sparsely-haired head wrapped in an ornate scarf that left the top of her scalp exposed. The ill-dry skin of Knyazhna emphasized the dark sockets in which her eyes were almost lost, and her cheeks buried in her bony framework. Jacob could feel that in a few more moments his face would express what he saw. He knew he must say something to water down the unpleasant thickness of the introduction. He recalled his earlier interest in Knyazhna's outfit and its color; now he understood it's importance. It was a subject he could talk about.

"Emerald green is a savior topic," he thought. "I love the color of your dress. Emerald green, I would say?" Jacob hoped the situation might improve.

"It is. Emerald green is the color of life," Knyazhna softly pronounced, "You may take your seat. I will shake your hand later." Knyazhna winked and smiled sweetly. Her top sharp teeth contrasted with a non-existent bottom row adding to the gut-churning moment. At his dismissal, Jacob smiled.

CHAPTER 4

JELLYFISH

In a flood of disgust, Jacob scurried back to his chair. Now he truly appreciated the fact that his seat was so far away from the revolting appearance of the elderly lady. But the sickening image of the nearly mummified Knyazhna stuck in Jacob's head and he was worried it might affect his appetite. His imagination seemed excessively vivid since he had entered the territory of the castle. "Perhaps it's just an impression from this unusual habitation?" he tried to reason. "It is quite different, even from what I was expecting."

All of a sudden, just before sitting down, he believed he heard someone else's thoughts and experienced a paranormally alarmed sensation.

Unfortunately, Jacob soon realized that someone actually was speaking to him and he felt quit disappointed to lose his invented supernatural talent.

The bone-chilling voice of old Knyazhna came from across the table, "And what did you expect? Your duty was clearly described: to perform the duty of a muse, not limited by being prepared for an extraordinary journey, for the completion of a novel. As well as the description of the employer: a temperamental, greatly mature Lady writer requires a young free-spirited cupid for inspiration of her creation. It is all in writing."

With his back still facing Knyazhna, Jacob stopped and spoke, "I think there was nothing said about preparing for an extraordinary journey. My contract said, not limited to pampering. And extraordinary was used when describing the writer."

"You think? We all read between words what we wish to be written. You must have missed a comma somewhere. Next time obtain advice from a lawyer," Knyazhna paused. "Next time my cupid."

Out of the corner of his eye, Jacob saw how Knyazhna was squinting and devilishly smiling at him. Jacob was not sure if he should turn and face her or pretend he did not hear Knyazhna's advice. He scratched his shoe heel against the floor, but it did not make a plausible distracting noise. He then grabbed a large fork and dropped it onto his silver plate.

Knyazhna burst into toothless whistling laughter,

"I appreciate your comedic acting skills. You do have a natural talent to entertain. I've missed that very much."

Jacob turned his body to face the laughing old witch, and whispered to himself, "Gee, I am just overanalyzing my own thoughts. I'm clearly exhausted." He finally took his seat and began to eat without looking anywhere else but his plate. The consumption of the feast went on in silence. For some time, Jacob, preoccupied with the servings of superb food and drinks, was kindly left alone. He loved the heavy silver forks and the tasty, firm bread. By all measures of the high standards of his spoiled demands of satisfaction Jacob collapsed into an agreeable state of being.

Regrettably, like a crack in a dam, old Knyazhna spoke again, "Tomorrow, we celebrate the finale of the 12th chapter of my novel, 'Excerptus - Child of Nosferatu'."

A very sudden tactile weight of actual physical pressure pressed upon Jacob's shoulders. It startled him, but then he recognized the distinctive marching of the servant.

"Gosh, You almost broke my neck. Your hands feel like lead weights. Are you a power lifter?" Jacob turned and saw that Bohdan, securely holding about 400 pages of the manuscript, stood about 10 feet behind. None of it had any explanation.

Knyazhna laughed again, like a child playing an

innocent trick on a friend, "A delicate, sensitive boy. The best kind."

There, in the corridor tunnel leading to the kitchen, where Knyazhna had earlier whispered to a shadowy tower, Jacob saw again, the tall moving Bohdan-like figure. Jacob gasped and turned around to find Bohdan still behind his chair. Jacob turned back and looked into the tunnel but now saw no one. Bohdan placed the hand written manuscript on the table in front of Jacob and pointed to the napkin resting on his lap.

"How many people are staying in this house?" Jacob asked intensely. He wiped his hands with the suggested napkin and began to flip through pages of the manuscript.

"Not another living soul. Only you," Bohdan replied.

"All right, very funny," Jacob laughed to cover his nervousness. "And who are those others, without souls?"

A prolonged silence filled the room. Digging in her plate loudly, Knyazhna pretended not to hear, not the questions nor answers. Jacob's awareness came back strongly, and his mind played suggestive possibilities of being captured by a psycho murderer or a dark-spirited, devil worshiping sect.

"Only you. As a guest, I mean," Bohdan smiled almost kindly.

Analyzing the servant's cunning demeanor, Jacob thought, "This sly one smiles as kind as a sneaky devil could probably muster." Releasing his crazy suspicion, he rationalized that the slightly extravagant communication of the hosts was affected by their reclusive existence.

Old Knyazhna seemed to enjoy the awkwardness of the interaction, as would a hawk freed from the imprisonment of a gilded cage into the open skies above soaring fields.

"That's not too funny. Boring in fact. Can any one do a better joke?" requested Jacob in a brighter mood. He wished for a relaxed nothing-to-do night and hoped that he would not be asked to read Knyazhna's scribblings, at least not today, the first day of his arrival. Jokingly, he joined his hands in prayer, as he had seen in the movies. In real worship, Jacob had no need nor experience.

Jacob flipped through a few pages then closed the manuscript patting the title page and expressed a compliment worthy of a LA based model. "Nice hand writing, 'Ex-cccc-erptus - Child of Nosferatu.' Ah okay,

'EXCERPTUS - Child of Nosferatu',"

Jacob finally put it together. "Preference in hand writing or computer illiterate?" As the words left his lips even he, a free-spirited hipster, found himself sounding rude. "It's kind of a joke. I mean you could also hire me as a typist. I am not a pro, but will do for this purpose".

"Handwriting is my Royal preference. As my hand is wired through my body to my mind, the paper with my words will connect with the world. I must, by necessity, touch a blank canvas," answered Knyazhna calmly,

"All you find in handwriting has been written by me."

Then she added, noticing Jacob's face lose interest, "I have no where to hurry to."

"Oh Yeah?" Jacob thought, "I would hurry if I were you and finish the story. You aren't a spring chicken anymore." Letting a breath out, he held back his sharp tongue "Its cool to be a writer. Makes sense living in such isolation. Imaginary world. I assume its a sci-fi, f, fiction?"

"Psychological suspense," Knyazhna answered and left her mouth opened after she chewed on something. She let her jaw relax to its natural fully opened position, exposing the darkness of the cavity. It was deep, like it had no end, like an eternity or a black hole that was about to swallow him.

From a distance, it reminded Jacob of that gloomy corridor that he walked through when he first entered the castle.

All of Jacob's observations cycled through his

mind as he was getting sleepy at the table. Yet, he supposed that this was not the end of the evening, so he must wake up. Jacob forced himself to add some fun phrases to his speech but his words did not come out right. The long travel, lack of sleep and the additional shock of meeting his employer was getting to him. Jacob was losing his ability to speak with his "free-style" kind of way and tried to make an impression of interest, "I see no recent pictures. I assume you don't have children of your own, Knyazhna?"

"Sadly children aren't what they should be to their parents these days, treating their old age and incapability as a burden," Knyazhna answered as if she was prepared for that specific question, "Young people seem to forget that from the first day of their life, their elder guardians not only understood but encouraged them to a world of discovery, while supporting them through a time of inability to defend themselves. To gain knowledge growing into life is not easy but how do you think it feels day-by-day, month to month to learn how to die?"

Jacob's young puppy look reminded Knyazhna to accept her usual disappointment of young people.

"No children? No pets?" Jacob asked once more.

Pleased by his question, she answered, "I keep a jellyfish."

"I would have expected something more fitting for a mystery writer in this withdrawn place. Like a black cat? A gold fish at least. But a jellyfish?" Jacob drank a big gulp of wine.

"A cat?" said Knyazhna sarcastically with a held look of concern, "Competition for my independence burdens me."

"Nice. I like your sense of humor, Your Majesty," replied a digestively satisfied Jacob.

Bohdan returned and neatly rearranged some things on the table. Though he was standing near by, Jacob clearly saw a Bohdan-like figure in the dark corridor leading to the kitchen.

"Wow!" Jacob blamed his own hallucination, "Is there any one else in the house right now? Servants, guests?"

"Just 'The Followers' at the moment," answered Bohdan calmly.

"Followers? What's that? Who are they? Students? Volunteers?" smirked Jacob.

"It is a name for the dark imprints of ourselves," explained Bohdan firmly.

"You mean your shadow?" In order to impress his new audience with his knowledge Jacob said, "Right, 'Followers' because a shadow follows you all the time. That's a cool name!"

"Not always," Bohdan responded.

And then Jacob could not believe his eyes as he watched Bohdan's 'Follower' on the floor. First, it stretched in size, then separated and finally moved away. Again, Jacob excused what he saw to his fatigue and nerves.

"The danger with a shadow is that, at some point, if it is given the opportunity under the power of the sun, it begins to shift and step forward, in front of the Master," unexpectedly intruded Knyazhna.

"That is why we don't let it see the sun, keeping it always subservient as a 'Follower'," added Bohdan.

Jacob gulped another full glass of the intoxicating red drink and his tongue moved on its own. "Well forgive me Bohdan, but you've been given too much time for expressing yourself. Aren't you a subservient servant? Ah forgive me, a 'Follower'? A Shadow?"

As the speech of the guest echoed around the room, Bohdan's face suddenly changed to a flaming skinned Devil ready to release its blood thirsty nature. Avoiding Bohdan, Jacob redirected his look at the kitchen corridor from where a dusty large shadow moved toward Bohdan's feet. It became smaller and finally hid behind him where it belonged.

To avoid revealing all of the secrets of the castle too soon, entertained and in high-spirit, Her Majesty Knyazhna sat back hiding her face behind the glow of the candle, "I admire cats. However, they are difficult to keep inside the premises. They would make me worried sick having them wondering around. Too many blood thirsty beasts outside that gate."

"Jellyfish then, ha?" trying to hide the shock of what he had seen, Jacob needlessly touched a few objects on the dining table and joked, "I take it that the taste for sweets and the quietness of fish are pleasing for a woman."

There was nothing in Knyazhna's facial expression that would indicate her understanding of Jacob wittiness, so she moved her lips.

One thing was clear to Jacob, his teasing in this company was badly ineffective. His mind summarized, "I guess it is excusable. It is like telling a joke to a Neanderthal about electricity. These people live with out electricity. That narrows it down to try to have fun with not much to tease about." Noticing his hosts continuous clueless stare, he use his charm, "Sweets as in jellies, jelly beans, jelly fish candies. To eat. Sweets." He was sure that she would figure this out.

Old Knyazhna Zoryana smiled sadly at Jacob's predictable intellect and kindly paused in her feedback. She stood up and slowly walked to the rounded glass fish aquarium. On one side, it was decorated with green seaweed plants growing from a small corral castle. On the other side lay a half dozen natural stones and many sea shells. Knyazhna scratched at the glass aquarium, "Jellyfish are not interested in shells. But shells serve an important function. They hold the sand."

Jacob did not care about the shells nor the sand that somehow needed to be protected in a fish tank, and he could not argue that fact with his limited knowledge of marine biology and oceanography that he picked up at Sea World when he was seven. He lifted his head up to the ceiling and then returned his gaze to the aquarium and said nothing.

The pile of small stones moved, and the jellyfish showed up like on the stage of cabaret with its tentacles spreading out as if it knew it was loved. What first appeared to be a colorless body, suddenly burst with color from its core. It held translucent hues of blue, red or God knows what color, but it had the vibrance of life. Vibrance that Knyazhna did not have to say the least.

Looking at the present reality through the fish tank, old Knyazhna directed her distorted cataractal eye at Jacob and whispered, "That magnificent creature profoundly inspires me."

"Now I am in competition with the jellyfish. I thought I am here to inspire you, my Ladyship?" Jacob relaxed his torso in sensual manner and shook his head in a silly way.

"You are a visual inspiration, Jacob. Purely." Knyazhna answered quietly and kissed at the jellyfish through the glass tank.

Jacob joyfully jumped up out of his seat, "Of course I am visual inspiration with my handsome face and awesome body." He got up and walked to the jellyfish reservoir, struck a pose and tried to compose a song, which came out as a bad plagiarism of something already bad, "Hey Jelly, Jelly, got no body to offer. It's all in a jelly form..." Before Jacob could say another ridiculous phrase, his feet slipped and he fell on the spot. Clumsily trying to get up, the drunken guest was helped and held by Bohdan.

"Jellyfish are much more than five percent matter," spoke Bohdan while he was removing Jacob to a safe distance from the jellyfish tank and guarding him from further silliness.

"Ahh that hurts," Jacob rubbed his hip.

"The jellyfish inspires me spiritually. Unlike humans," the pupils of Knyazhna's eyes became bigger, eventually almost conquering the entire territory of the white part of her eyes. Beginning in a weak posture but slowly gaining strength, Knyazhna breathed out heavily, "It is an extraordinary immortal organism. Once it finishes its reproductive frame, it doesn't age or die. Contrary to humankind, it falls into the deepest seclusion and reverts itself back into its sexually immature stage."

"Right. The same happens to an old person, doesn't it?" Jacob said pointing out Knyazhna's winter of life. Insisting on an independent position, Jacob pulled from the steadying arm of Bohdan, but slipped and landed back on the floor. Bohdan did not bother to catch him.

Pessimistically, without any apparent reaction, Knyazhna continued to educate her easy going short memory pupil, "There, in the lowest darkness, its cells convert into their earliest form, stem cells. A stem cell can become anything, even an 'egg cell', an unfertilized mature female reproductive cell or a spermatozoon, a male reproductive cell. The fusion of these two types of cells are meant to produce a fertilized egg or ovum and form a new organism," Knyazhna delivered with breath taking admiration then paused her breathing for a moment.

Jacob felt uncomfortable listening about baby making from an old woman and thought "Perhaps the old witch has an intimate interest in me? I hope not." Then shouted, "I hope not!"

Knyazhna finally inhaled and continued, "From there, the fertilized egg starts the cycle of growth all over again leading to infinite life. That kind of transformation is unseen in the mammal world." Knyazhna touched the aquarium and looked closely through the curved glass of the reservoir, that magnified the immortal creature inside. "Her name is Turritopsis Nutricula." Knyazhna gazed at the jellyfish with an expression of both worship and envy.

To change the sexual topic, Jacob bravely stood up and reinserted his wittiness, "Nutricula, like Dracula?"

Ignoring the nonsense and flair of her simpleton guest, Knyazhna continued, "It has no blood."

"It sounds like an ideal dream transformation for

anybody," Jacob lowered his voice to sound more mature.

"There is one complexity," hastily responded Knyazhna.

At the brink of falling asleep while standing, Jacob blinked at her.

"This phenomenal creature is incredibly simple that it has no brain," explained Knyazhna and then made a loud moaning noise. They looked at each other for a while.

Severely fighting boredom and avoiding further Jellyfish talk, Jacob expressed his fake interest, "So, you were saying your novel is about children vampires?"

"It is not about children but a Child."

"Okay one child." Jacob repeated his own interpretation of what she said.

"It is not about someone giving a life." Knyazhna firmly stated. "Not new born, but one born anew, into a different world."

"Okay. Like reborn? Cool I like that kind of stuff. I get it, so who is the novel about?" Jacob asked with actual curiosity.

"I would call it autobiographical," Knyazhna smiled as if this was a joke.

"Ha, ha, ha," Jacob answered with the skill of a bad actor. Realizing that this was not a proper response, he walked straight to the table and stuffed a chunk of meat into his mouth.

"My request, which is mandatory for my inspiration; is that you speak your thoughts as close to the truth as possible. Even if they will disturb my pride," Knyazhna politely announced.

Understanding that he must speak Jacob spat out. "I can begin anytime. Right now if you wish?"

Knyazhna gestured to him to go on with his truth, while Bohdan poured wine into Jacob's half-empty glass.

"Thank you," said Jacob, then delivered with abundant audacity, "Not to be rude Knyazhna but your servant looks less exhausted than you do and he is the one who busts his butt."

Knyazhna took a sip of her drink and a large thick red drop ran down her chin, "I like to keep them fresh and on a leash in hope for eternal life. Until I no longer need them, of course." The white silk cloth which she used to wipe her face, became red.

"Hah!" exclaimed Jacob as if he was expecting that exact answer. "So you use them, lie to them and then discard them?"

"Mostly, they lie to me by promising their

obedience to their master, to me, with all their heart. But then, I find out they have no heart," Knyazhna breathed spasmodically.

"And how do you find out, Your Ladyship? Do you carve it out with a knife through their chest? Ha, ha, ha!" laughed Jacob feeling lightheaded and pleased that conversation between them had became more engaging.

Bohdan's rosy cheeks suddenly turned pale hinting to Jacob that he had gone too far.

"This one," Knyazhna pointed at Bohdan. "Bohdan, admires me, for now. I feel obligated for his sincerity toward me. Therefore, I reward him with my attention."

Getting drunk, Jacob rambled quietly, "I guess, if there is no one around for hundreds of miles," then he ended the sentence in a non-coherent mumble, "A, m, a..."

"I enjoy our involved conversation. However, I am not tolerant toward anyone's familiarity," Knyazhna's voice echoed all over the hall, "For the time of your employment, you must honor me as a Lady. Or you will travel back penniless."

"So what about your request my Lady?" asked Jacob, "Of saying the truth, which I assume is anything I think openly."

"You can tutor your thinking to be respectful,

Jacob," answered Knyazhna with almost maternal gentleness. She stood up and recited,

"To know the price of youth is wealth. Youth itself is a best seller: it requires no talent nor noble qualities, nor royal blood, because it is not affected by social change. It knows no other. The movingly expressive Youth is the only power that rules by sincere ignorance and arrogance, in order to reach what is wished. Unfortunately, when humans finally collect the comprehension of it, they are far beyond the border of rejuvenation."

Knyazhna wetted an additional white silk napkin with the thick red liquid and wiped her fingers. "Now you will take a bath, my boy."

Jacob swallowed with difficulty as if he had a hard candy stuck in his throat and said, "Wow! How fun!" Then he rumored in his thought, "The orders begin. I guess it is for the best, how much conversation can one really expect with a women old enough to be your great-grandmother and in the presence of a servant with his foreboding dreariness. How much at all? Nothing in common, nothing to share, nothing to smile about. But this is happening and I'm here to make it possible. Hopefully, I can handle all of it."

CHAPTER 5

HAPPY DREAMS

EUROPEAN CASTLE, BATHROOM – NIGHT

Wrapped in towels and a woolen blanket, Jacob walked into the corridor of the bathing room. He removed his wrap, hung it on a hook and proceeded to the main washing area, which to say was large, was an understatement. A few thick candles on the wall were blinking calmly.

To the right of the entrance, a very long wooden bench was situated. A couple yards further, on the same side, sat two large wooden barrels. Jacob walked in and checked the barrels, they were filled with hot and cold water. Deeper in on the other side, was rooted a coal fed fireplace with an attached supply brick bin. Jacob moved closer to inspect in more detail. The fireplace looked more like a cooking stove with its four walls made of stone. It was topped by an iron plate with two round openings covered with interlocking iron rings forming a lid for access. On the surface of the iron plate sat an enormous cast cooking pot with boiling water producing hot steam. Right in front of the fireplace stood a large permanent stool made of stone, similar to the stove. The room appeared to be something in between a Turkish 15th century "Hamam" and a traditional Russian "Banya." In any case, the place was well heated and full of steam.

Jacob returned back, and as any good American might, chose the oversized bench. He sat, stretched his legs forward and tilted his head back exposing the front of his neck. He inhaled with pleasure and opened his towel, "Awesome! It is too good. I knew there was someone up there watching over me so I could make it here. Such a beautiful body couldn't die for nothing." Then, spreading his arms and legs wider in bliss, he whispered, "But damn, I wasn't sure I would make it through that exhausting conversation with that old witch. Thank God it ended."

"I would not do that," Bohdan's voice sounded startlingly near.

Jacob covered his front and sat up, "What? I just said 'Thank God'."

"And that too," said Bohdan from behind, coming out of the darkness, "Be careful to expose your neck in unknown settings."

"Why? Will a vampire attack me?" Jacob answered with sarcasm and in that single moment he lost all the buzzing goodness that was running through his body. He was still comforted by the warmth but with the return of the soberness, the feeling of the security in the grand castle drifted away like a nocturnal animal howl in the wind. Suddenly, an owl was heard through the castle's walls, hooting her monotone sadness.

"You never know, something sharp might fall on the fine skin of your neck," said Bohdan and pointed up. There above the bench, ran a metal pole on which hung all kinds of sharp metal implements, including spears for moving coal. The owl's hoot changed to a growl. A wing-flapping noise landed near the small window of the bathing room. The following cries sounded like a few birds at once. Both men were quiet for a moment.

"Sounds like a dove, no, a cuckoo bird cooing. I watched a documentary on it, on the way here. It's some kind of free bird tramp. Can you imagine, it lays her eggs and leaves them. I thought it was an owl at first but then I remembered," excited, Jacob voiced his semi knowledgeable expertise.

"Oh, but it was," answered Bohdan. "More importantly, the cooing is ready to be counted."

"Didn't you just say it was an owl?" asked Jacob.

Ignoring the question the servant continued, "Have you ever heard any of the Eastern European 'Skazanya' tales about the cuckoo bird's foretelling?"

Jacob smirked, "What can a crazy cuckoo's cuckoldry possibly mean? Oh, sorry, I forgot that everything, and especially crazy things, means something important over here." Jacob shrugged and spat out the core of the fruit he was nibbling on.

Bohdan walked to the fireplace and with a spear-tipped coal poker 'kocherga', he very skillfully removed the interlocking iron rings from the top access holes, "If you listen to the cooing and count the coos, you will know exactly how much time you have left of your life." Then with a small shovel he threw plenty of coal into the opening. The burning flame reflected red on Bohdan's face, in a very unnatural way. It seemed as if all of his skin became blood red. Upon closing the last iron ring of the stove, Bohdan's appearance had returned to normal.

In disbelief Jacob closed then opened his eyes, "Why should I take it on my account? Why do you think its cooing for me? How do I know it is not cooing for you, Bohdan?"

"It does not coo for me anymore. I know exactly how long I have," Bohdan answered with a pretentious crafty stretched smile.

To Jacob, it was a familiar facial expression. That kind of smile he had seen in Los Angeles many times when people don't really mean to be personal or sincere, but they do it anyway because it is easier to smile than explain their indifference to the situation.

"Ask the bird," advised Bohdan, "Just say, how much time do I have left of my life?"

"That is ridiculous. Why would I put my fate into a beak of a crazy Cuckoo bird?" Jacob tentatively drank his wine, "I don't even believe in this, your European fairy tale, stuff."

"Well, if you don't believe, then why would you be afraid of asking?" inquired the servant, placing a cooked dove on the silver tray next to Jacob. "It is really tasty, have you tried it before?"

In frustration, Jacob ate the dove and loved it. The cooing continued, first slow and then more often. "Can we shut the damn bird up!"

"It is waiting for the question, otherwise we will have to shoot it dead," Bohdan replied with amused laughter.

"Fine, you son of an old witch!" hurriedly shouted Jacob toward the window, "How much time do I, Jacob, have left of my life?!"

The silence sat heavily in the air for few seconds, then the cooing began, "Coo, cu, Coo..." The first few coos left Jacob breathlessly anxious.

Then as cooing continued, he felt his heart was skipping a few beats, "Cu, Coo, Cu, Coo, Cu, Coo, cu, Coo, cu, Coo... Cu," the stop of the last coo made Jacob's heart pause and even for one who didn't believe in such things, he felt nauseous.

"It's only fourteen!" inhaled and exhaled Jacob, "What does it mean?"

"It could be fourteen years, fourteen months, fourteen weeks, fourteen days, fourteen hours or fourteen minutes," Bohdan answered stoically.

"That is crazy mathematics!" sounding on the edge assessed Jacob. "There's a big bloody big difference between fourteen years and fourteen minutes!" Jacob glared at his watch to ascertain the exact time.

In contrast to Jacob's fidgety uneasy disposition, Bohdan did not say anything; he just stood there emotionless and unmoving.

"I knew it was crazy to ask a crazy bird. This entire place is mad and demented!" shouted Jacob. "That is very funny! It is not funny at all! I might die in 14 minutes," he laughed into his silver goblet in between gulps of wine.

"I doubt the correctness of my answer. You may better ask the bird," Bohdan's words came out like an icy wind creating a tiny puffs of fog.

Jacob wiped his eyes and the puffs were gone, "Sure, I will. Where is that crazy thing?" Jacob jumped up and rushed to a tiny narrow window that looked more like a split in the wall. Having trouble opening the rusty lock of the window's shutters, he pulled many times then screamed and finally yanked it open. As he did, wide-open yellow eyes forcefully stared at him from a white feathery body. "What the...!" Jacob jumped back. There, in the window frame sat a large owl. He stared back at it determined to find something. He finally noticed the snake-like almond shaped eyes that were very unnatural for a bird, "It's not even a cuckoo bird." Jacob took an unbalanced step back and tripped.

"It is a Snowy Owl," Bohdan interrupted him. "And extremely rare..."

"Whatever it is," Jacob interrupted him back. "I will not leave this spot for 15 minutes!" He fearfully took another step back, falling onto the bench. The bench shook an adjacent column, which held one end of the horizontal metal pole, and had made the hanging implements clank loudly.

Jacob looked up above him at the swaying tools. "It was not even a cuckoo," he hysterically laughed hiding his cry.

"It was not," reiterated Bohdan as he poured hot and cold water for Jacob's washing needs.

Jacob followed the arrow of his watch silently for a few minutes then uncontrollably exclaimed once again, "It was a crazy owl, pretending to be a cuckoo, trying to kill me! Another witch, like all crazy women!"

"Oh no, this is a male, who mostly preys on lemming..."

"Layman," repeated Jacob.

"I suppose it is possible. Pardon my accent, I meant lemmings, a small animal like a rat." For a brief moment Bohdan waited on Jacob's reaction, then continued, "A Snow Owl female is much more vicious. Once, I watched one in her nest surrounded by her little fluffy juveniles. Her white face was covered with fresh blood, that of her own feeblest chick. She tore its flesh off and fed it to the healthy ones."

Jacob's lower jaw dropped to its physiologically maximum extended position. He began to see bright red on the white feathers around the owl's beak.

The fearfully vivid imagination on Jacob's face was clearly noticeable to Bohdan and he asked, "Should I close the window?"

"No! After fifteen minutes pass, I will kill that ugly bird," said Jacob focusing his gaze on the Snowy Owl, which was still sitting on the dry tree branch next to the window frame.

The owl quacked with its eagle beak, "krek-krek" and then made a short sound resembling a dog's bark. Bohdan silently began to walk away toward the exit.

"Where are you going Bohdan? Come back immediately. You're a coward. That thing is waiting for my end."

"Do you wish me to lock the window?" Bohdan asked.

"No!" he shouted.

"I am right here, just getting more..." Bohdan did not bother to finish his sentence and returned from the far corner with wine. They sat looking at each other, Jacob at the owl, Bohdan at Jacob.

"Fourteen minutes have passed," Bohdan commented.

"One more minute longer," whispered Jacob. That one minute went on for a very long time as Jacob thought back on his life, and sadly found absolutely nothing was imprinted by his 'ordinary genius'. Not art, not family who would remember him in remorse, no kind deeds for the sake of the unprofitable kindness, not even a decent dream written on a piece of paper. Worthless words, meaningless places, strangers and indulgence of self idolization, was all that was left behind. There were a few portfolio albums, but they exposed nothing but poses. Not one of the pictures showed his inner self worth which Jacob knew he had. Trying to fit in to the demands of fast modern coolness, his own free spirited style was not free from the fashionable Hollywood social stigma.

"Fifteen minutes have passed, sir," Bohdan reminded, "May we continue our activities and assignments? Would you like to relax and wash yourself?" He stood up to move on with his errands.

"No!" Jacob raised up with the anger of his dented ego, "I demand to punish that accursed bird."

"I do not see that as a necessity. This is a rare species, sir. And truly, the bird did not harm you. You just tripped."

"I don't think so. That thing wanted me to die!" Jacob required in the form of a question, "Do you have a gun?"

The white owl outside the window blinked at Jacob a few times.

"No guns, but there is a sword right at your hand, sir," Bohdan pointed to the sharp sword that hung above Jacob.

In a rush for revenge, Jacob extended his hand up but failed to properly grab the weapon. Seemingly in slow motion yet in a high speed pulse of reality, Jacob simultaneously fell back as the sword swung down. Instinctively, he yanked his legs apart as the tip of the sword penetrated the towel micro-distant from his frontal pride, thrusting deep into the wooden bench.

The owl growled, shrieked then took off spreading his wings like a hawk. "Eccentric bird, that is," Bohdan's eyes followed the owl's departure, while he nonchalantly pulled out the sword from between Jacob's thighs.

Slowly gathering his legs together, Jacob hugged his knees and cried, "Why would someone hang that nasty rubbish up there, above a seat where people suppose to bathe, relax, not to feel like you are at a guillotine shop?"

"For one, you must always be careful. One can never be too careful," Bohdan said in a friendly tone, "Not less important, is that where you are sitting, sir, is not the place to wash." He pointed forward to the permanent bathing stone stool, "There, next to the fireplace, is a seat that is meant for bathing as it is easier to reach the hot and cold water."

"Why are you here, anyway?" Jacob asked looking else where.

From a servant's position, Bohdan's spoke with ease, "To assist our guests in a premises that they are not familiar with. And to protect dear guests like you, sir Jacob, from unknown situations." He firmly, held Jacob's arm and walked him to the single seat washing area, "For those who are not used to the darkness, this particular place may appear dangerous."

"Great, thanks I can manage from now on," Jacob pulled his arm from Bohdan's strong grasp and fixed his towel that was slipping down his hips.

"I will make sure you stay warm for as long as you must," said Bohdan while he threw coal into the fireplace through a small side door. As he did, the burning fire again reflected bloody red onto one side of Bohdan's face while utter darkness engulfed the other side.

"Am I seeing Satan?" Jacob thought. But he had no idea what Satan should look like except from simplified drawings he remembered in comic books and exaggerated characters in Hollywood films. "Brrr," he shivered and plunged his head into the barrel of cold water. When he emerged from under the sobering liquid, Bohdan was gone.

The soft sound of one word came from beyond the door, "Enjoy."

Without time to fully decipher the word, Jacob's mind raced, "I hope Old Knyazhna will not touch me tonight. Tomorrow I'm gone. This place is nothing but medieval poison. All of it, from the tiniest spec of soil to the..., which holds this multi-chambered tombstone." A dull echoing noise webbed across the walls of the bathing room, and Jacob suspected he was not alone, "I must relax to gain strength. Tonight I'll rest, calm down and climb to clarity out of this bizarre situation." Jacob placed his arms up to his elbows in the barrel of cold water, "I hope the water in here is just water." He stared for a while into the barrel and the sounds of water drops coming from his forehead sounded reverberated and distant. A swift draft of cold air ran through the room, then quietness came. Jacob truly enjoyed the rest of the washing. He used hand-crafted soap all over his body and head. It smelled like lavender and pear, a strange combination that he absolutely loved. After washing off the suds, he slid soap over his skin again and again, then rinsed once more.

EUOPEAN CASTLE, BEDROOM – AFTER MIDNIGHT

It was after midnight by the time Jacob gently wiggled his feet under the warm blanket. He pulled the white sheets closer to his face and smelled the unexpected fresh and familiar aroma of lavender. As if he was writing a letter to a good friend, he quietly began to describe the interior design of the Victorian-furnished room assigned to him for his stay in the castle.

"My bed, comfy and king worthy. A night table and lamp, I imagine it's a kerosene one, cause it smells, but it doesn't bother me. Quite the opposite, it is calming. The small mirror's gilding matches my taste. There are heavy expensive fabric curtains over the windows and behind it are closed shutters. Love it! And a writing table, not sure if I am going to use it, still, it's pleasant to look at. The door looks very secure."

The door to the bedroom did appear to be very strong. It was secured with an inner lock made of heavy iron. Before getting into bed Jacob made sure he locked it. Then he double checked it again. He pushed the iron lock up and down a dozen times obsessively. Only a day ago, Jacob would not have believed that he would behave this way. Yet, when certain experience crosses someone's life, they become less fearless and less trusting. The kerosene lamp gave off a small but enjoyable wavy glow. Jacob whispered something and quickly crossed himself which was a hundred percent out of character. He then dimmed the light, settled more into the pillow and closed his eyes like a sweet baby bear. As he fell into the deep space of sleep, he heard the squeak of the door opening.

"Who is it?"

There in the doorway, Her Majesty old Knyazhna Zoryana stood in a white sleeping gown. Very sweetly, almost as if asking permission she whispered, "I came to tuck you in, little cub, and I brought you a bed time story."

Jacob's eyes popped open to the point of falling out. "How did you open the door? Do you have a key? I checked it so many times to be sure it was locked."

"You might have tried so many times that you left it unlocked. A tired mind can play tricks on itself," she smiled at him like a kind-hearted grandmother.

"I guess so. I am very tired, can't tell," Jacob was not sure what most puzzled him: that he left the door unlocked, that Knyazhna opened it or that the old woman was standing in his room in her night gown. The old Majesty looked nothing like any of the ladies he had comforted and entertained before. They weren't all young by any means. Most pushed the upper side of middle age, but even then, they were all so well taken care of that a younger girl would look like a wandering gypsy in comparison. His previous mature clients had always excited him and never induced repulsion. Liz Wartz was an exception and not only due his code of principles. Jacob never forgot his vengeful boss Liz. Recalling their break on the yacht, he saw all clearly now. Liz was not only making an immense profit on his assignment, she was also punishing Jacob by pimping him to someone two feet out of the grave. Liz had taken him from the splendor of Hollywood and dumped him into this world of medieval brutality.

As Knyazhna slowly took little steps toward the bed, Jacob tried to push her away with his recently formed power of imagination. He saw her coming closer, so he pictured her starting again at the doorway. He successfully tried a few times, but in reality old Knyazhna was still making tiny steps toward him. Feeble Knyazhna reached Jacob, her sly destination, and surprisingly jumped onto his bed. Gently pushing him to one side, she laid the manuscript on his legs just above his knees. Sitting up, Knyazhna began to pet his head.

Jacob lay horizontally with his blanket almost covering his face. His eyes began to rush side to side in embarrassment. At first, he wanted to go completely under the blanket, but his vivid imagination of what might happen if he couldn't see the old witch made him reconsider. Oddly, at that moment, Jacob remembered himself as a child, hiding under his baby quilt, allowing only his eyes to see and control the situation of his fright. As long as the quilt was firmly tucked all around his body 'all was all right'. That feeling of safety from his childhood, made him want to repeat similar actions. Unfortunately, he was aware he had to act like an adult, so he pulled himself out from under the blanket to a half-sitting position. Exposing his chest, he leaned back against the head board and picked up the manuscript, 'Excerptus - Child of Nosferatu'.

Jacob began reading, as duty called,

> *"All humans die. All creatures die. Everything on Earth and outside of it has an end. The whole entirety perishes or changes its form into something else in the harmonious system of the universe but the name of the finale, that comes one way or another, is simply Death. The Living can not easily say goodbye to their short lives so they seek to prolong their existence. Humans and animals and plants give birth to offspring, cloning micro parts of themselves to ensure continuity and portray their likeness. But none of the offspring can inherit the feelings of memories or desires, even of the most common events. Artists leave their creation in the form of art, which is their eternal footprint. Scientists dig into the*

ancient to progress our comprehension of the unidentified. They expand technological progress and thereby keep their names echoing forever in the universe. But none of it is really them anymore.

Yet, Nosferatu remain the same as when they were human, except for their new unfeelingness to excitement. They have seen all, they have felt all, they hoped for much as humans, and they were disappointed in all of its dismay. However, they decide to stay.

Signed, Her Majesty Knyazhna Zoryana."

During the reading, bursting in between heat and freezing chills, Jacob frequently paused to breathe. He was trying not to move from his spot until the end of the paragraph, as he stopped his jaw finally locked together drowning him with the panic of a permanent inability to speak.

Old Knyazhna, seemingly pleased with Jacob's reading, was making herself comfortable as would a small child listening to a bedtime story from a parent.

Jacob physically felt Knyazhna push herself closer

and closer to him. She laid her head on his chest breathing against it with her icy breath. Fighting to overcome his repugnance toward his closeness to the life-limited body of Knyazhna, Jacob's abdominal muscles tightened up resulting in the relief of pressure in his facial muscles. Cold large drops of sweat flashed across his face, and his jaw finally relaxed. Being observant of his own body like this was beyond foreign to Jacob.

In spite of the old woman's inappropriate behavior, he liked the majority of what he saw and read. He forced himself to excuse and understand Knyazhna as a lonely person, who was losing her mind from the old age falling into a childhood stage perhaps like her jellyfish did. Jacob adjusted his position to move a few inches further away from Knyazhna and finished reading, "Signed, Her Majesty Knyazhna Zoryana. Do you sign every page that way?" he asked trying to loosen up. Yet something warned him very strongly to mistrust his employer.

Knyazhna squinted her eyes lustrously, "I mark all that is important to me. All that leaves my hands after I agree to it. Otherwise it's mine only." Knyazhna's cataract eye seemed to penetrate Jacob with its jelly-gaze.

As much as physical contact with Knyazhna sickened Jacob, he suddenly saw in her the look of a lost child or maybe an ugly orphan, someone who was hungry for care and warmth. "What a dreadfully aged stage of ugliness, yet in need of love as well," he thought. Only having the chance to observe her in a few moods and not being sure of what to expect from the sly old lady, Jacob was unsure about displaying his sympathy and susceptibility.

For some time, Knyazhna's behavior exhibited none of Jacob's suspicions. Jacob made a few more efforts to focus on the pages of the manuscript, but while reading the next sentence, he found himself back at the beginning of a previous one. He could no longer battle his delirious sleepiness, "I am very tired. I don't think I can do anymore reading."

"Then it is time for sweet dreams," Knyazhna charmingly agreed with her head on Jacob's chest. In that instant, his eyelids closed heavily.

CHAPTER 6

PRECIOUS VISITOR

A few moments after Jacob descended into sleep, he felt soothing easiness on his chest as if the old Knyazhna was not around. Blissfully, he moved side-to-side prepping his pillow, then wrapping his face in the down blanket. Several times throughout the night, half-awake, he opened his eyes in blurriness expecting haunting shadows and sounds but found nothing to be afraid of; he fell instantly asleep. The sensation of a snug, fluffy aura created a smile on his face, returning it to its natural appearance. At one point, the smell of kerosene was overwhelming to his sensitive nose, so he reached over to turn off the lamp.

There, standing at the doorway, as if out of focus, was a young girl dressed in a light as a snowflake white gown. Her posture conveyed the impression that she was closer to adulthood, perhaps nineteen. Confused, instead of observing the young beauty, Jacob visually examined the fabric of her dress, "It must be chiffon or lace. It is incredible." Jacob blinked once. She emerged right by his bed. For a moment Jacob froze, then thought, "What if Knyazhna is near by? What would she say if she discovers I have a visitor? What if they are not on friendly terms?" Frightened as a teenager bringing a girlfriend home to his room without his parents' permission, Jacob suddenly felt anxious.

His mind screamed for proof that Knyazhna was not nearby. He touched around his bed and looked at the locked door. "Well perhaps Knyazhna's visit was a dream?" Jacob concluded when he felt an uncomfortable pressure like a cut on his leg under the blanket. Tangled in his sheets was the manuscript. A tiny paper cut imprinted his blood onto one of the pages. "I must have been reading to Knyazhna and, when I fell asleep, she left."

Jacob waited a moment and began to acquaint himself with the graceful visitor, who was supposedly expecting his attention by staring at him. He extended his hand to touch the fabric of her dress, "Where did you come from? Who are you?"

The girl in snowflake chiffon giggled and took a few steps back toward the door, as her delicate dress swung forward.

"Don't leave!" he intensely whispered, "Stay,

please." Jacob offered his hand and hoped she would understand his friendly intent, "I am no one to be afraid of, no danger can come from me."

A frail shadow appeared behind the feminine body of the graceful visitor. A sound of dripping liquid was heard from a distance. Jacob moved in his bed in attempt to get up as he saw the shadow of his fragile guest becoming more dense until it indented itself into the wooden door. The dripping sound became closer and annoyed Jacob's ears. Jacob rapidly closed and opened his eyes. The shadow was gone but a remnant of the sound rattled softly. Jacob deduced, "The bathing and the draft affected me for sure."

The visitor in chiffon smiled softly, stepped forward and sat next to him on the bed. Her presence was an escape from all the gloominess of the estate. Jacob watched her fingers wandering under the blanket, it amused him. The lifted eyebrows of his fun visitor seemed to indicate that she had detected some kind of gem. With one yank she pulled out the manuscript and threw it into the air. The pages were dancing and landing like tree leaves in Autumn.

"Ah I thought you were trying to get under my sheets," Jacob optimistically said, but was not pleased with his simple joke that contradicted his earlier promise of not to offend. Luckily, she did not seem to be effected and remained in the same cheerful mood.

She poured a glass of wine and handed it to Jacob who eagerly drank it. Leaning forward, she licked droplets of wine from his dry lips.

Jacob shivered. He could not and, in fact, did not want to control his desires. At first, he barely touched her hand and then, when she did not move away gently gazing at him, he brushed her hair with his fingers. Tenderly hugging her, he hoped to have her around as a reward for his unfortunate position. She expressed a childish frown when she felt Jacob's gentleness growing into passion and pulled his hands away. Jacob held his breath then let it out slowly as if to not scare away a butterfly. She was, in comparison to all else that surrounded him, a fragile and dainty butterfly.

Not knowing what to expect from his beautiful guest who still had not said a word, Jacob began to sing a calming lullaby that he had learned from his mother when he was six. Because he had never heard it again, Jacob only recalled a small part of the song, so he continued repeating the little bit that he knew. It looked like singing had a positive influence on his precious visitor. She tilted her head to one side and mumbled something as if trying to follow the melody. Struggling to keep himself calm, Jacob needed to fill his lungs with air. In that micro-moment while he was inhaling, she suddenly climbed onto the bed and straddled his abdomen. Sliding lower, she positioned herself to a very agreeable physical area for Jacob.

Fearing that rising and falling of his chest might show his trembling emotions, Jacob began to breath with his abdomen, as he learned in a voice class during his few years of infrequently attending college.

However, his breathing turned to gasps and became obvious in revealing his desires. After a few more moments, the hands of his dainty impressionable visitor pulled away the blanket that separated their bodies.

She lifted herself up and sat back down. Then she tilted her head back and then forward to connect their foreheads. Jacob kissed her shoulders through the snow-light gown a few times. His lips wandered the texture of the fabric and thought, "It is strange to be fixated on fabric when this close to a young beauty in a foreign continent." Back home, Jacob would have hardly had any interest in clothes or fabrics. He would have ripped them off and tossed them aside from his sight in the throws of passion.

"What is so fascinating about this girl?" he wondered as his lips moved up to her exposed neck, "Perhaps it's her silence in combination with perfect understanding. Or her easiness in connecting with a foreign drifter, while I'm sure being exceptionally selective. I don't think I have ever considered any woman's viewpoint while being with them."

Jacob determined that she, a complete stranger, the dream of his every erotic fantasy, was perfect for him. He felt a rush all over his body as they became one. Her sexual determination for climax was as selfish as any young man. This was extremely attractive to Jacob. Her body moved in circles, up and down, and when she wiped her hair in his face it did not distract him. Jacob wanted it all to last forever, so to prolong his explosion he held out as long as possible.

For the first time in his life, Jacob watched the ecstasy of youth from the view point of a mature person. Not that he was much older than her but he began to decipher things with a tint of wisdom, "Is this what the cougar ladies feel when I burst my finale into them?" He paused his pondering when her lips ran across his hairless chest. This set him off in an uncontrollable moment. The outburst of his physical as well as emotional heightened state could not be compared to any earthly sensation he had ever experienced before. He stared out into nowhere while he climaxed again and again.

Gradually, Jacob returned from his euphoric selfishness. To exhibit his sublime infatuation with her, he reached up to kiss her lips with closed eyes.

He felt coldness; something rough and cracked surrounding her mouth. Jacob pulled back and slowly focused his vision. In spasms of revulsion he discovered old Knyazhna Zoryana sitting on top of him. He screamed and woke up.

Drenched in sweat, Jacob fearfully inspected his room from his bed. He heard a rooster wail and saw the morning rays of lighter sky through tiny cracks in the shutters. He climbed off the bed and walked toward the window to open the curtains and shutters. In the darkness he stepped on something that made a whooshing sound. Letting the daylight in, he saw under his feet, strewn over the floor the pages of the manuscript. He picked up one, it was the title page.

Jacob read, "Excerptus - Child of Nosferatu." In aspiration that his encounter with the enchanted visitor in chiffon was not a dream, he boyishly jumped back into bed and fell asleep almost instantaneously.

CHAPTER 7

GOOD DARK MORNING

EUROPEAN CASTLE, LIVING ROOM – NIGHT

Supplemented by a healthy burst of life in each and every one of his muscles, Jacob stretched his arms and legs and exited his room ecstatically. An urgent need to move with speed rushed through his body, yet, the darkness of the corridors became a major obstacle as he did not want to risk damaging himself. Then he recalled the strange European household rules. Not that the occupants were too snobbish, like he had seen in films about England, but there was something pretentiously aristocratic in their behavior. Instead of running, Jacob walked with large strides all the way down the main corridor and enjoyed it. From his hazy recollection of last night, he did not remember the way being that extensive, but took it as it was. He felt eager to eat, to see the other inhabitants of the castle and even to be entertained by their dark jokes. Before turning into an inner balcony that led to the stairway, he noticed the towering silhouette in the darkest corner.

"Hey Bohdan! Playing trick or treat?" Jacob jovially called out to the indistinct figure. The ghostly form dissolved with a sound of a swish. Addressing the dark empty corner, Jacob tried to hide the sensation of chills running down his spine by announcing optimistically, "Okay then, I will search this creepy house and I will find your hidden passages and moving walls Bohdy!"

Hurried by his growling stomach and thirst, Jacob eventually saw a trickle of light at the end of the corridor. In the process of turning into the inner balcony his hand came in contact with something slimy on the balcony rail. Jacob flicked his fingers and smelled something familiar. As it landed on the floor, he kicked it then saw it was a mushroom. "The cook, who ever it is, must have lost it. Maybe they dry them on the roof or how should I know what the crazies do with them?" he said to himself to justify the presence of the fungus being in such an unexpected area of the house.

From upstairs, Jacob could observe the living room that was perfectly set up for the banquet. His uncontrollable hunger forced him to dismiss all the disruptions and he rushed down the stairs. Reaching the table, he spent a few long seconds studying the feast and immediately singled out the cheese and crackers. There was no one around. He sat down and helped himself to a large slice of cheese, a few crackers, and a few pieces of baked duck. Stuffing it all into his mouth, he looked around like a thief not wanting to be caught red-handed. Handmade, fatty, creamy and crunchy, it all tasted out of this world. He chased it down with a handful of grapes.

Spreading his legs Jacob sat back and imagined himself as a peasant in a linen outfit sitting on hay and eating cloth-wrapped homemade food, "Strange, I have never experienced the lunch of a peasant. Where is that coming from? Maybe from my past life? No! I couldn't be a peasant. I must have seen it on the History Channel or something. Never mind." Jacob poured himself a glass of wine, smelling the consistency of the bottle's contents as if he was a wine connoisseur. He was not big on reading, yet in order to impress the clients in his secondary occupation as an escort, he had learned how to present himself from watching movies.

Eloquently carrying a glass of wine, rehearsing a performance that he had learned in acting class, Jacob stepped onto the outside balcony. He inhaled, filling the reservoir of his lungs deeply as if it was the last gasp of a desert wanderer in expectation of a dust storm. Scanning the far-spread land without its visible end, Jacob was reminded of The Pacific Ocean, "Like a shore less ocean seen from a distant cruise ship."

From that very position, endorsing the green

wilderness that pleasantly appeared existing independently of human activity, Jacob made up his mind to finally accept his occupation. He watched the nature joyfully. Passively traveling clouds began to close off the sun. A wall of fog suddenly rose up from the ground, quickly spreading to dissolve the surrounding landscape. Disregarding his previous nightmares and the change in weather, Jacob was melting in indulgence inside the seemingly, at the moment, safe castle walls. Abruptly, the muscles on his back contracted and pulled at his neck like someone had yanked him. The sound of heavy breathing vibrated in his ears. Jacob turned around and saw Knyazhna Zoryana standing far in the shadows of the living room.

Jacob felt uncomfortable, as if something inappropriate had happened between him and old Knyazhna.

The subconscious panic that he had witnessed wrongdoing on her part and now must beg for his life assuring his silence even under torture, unknowingly attacked him. "That's a bit over the top. When I'm in her presence, I feel nervous, unfit or under suspicion for a crime? But she is the one who is unfit in appearance and she is most likely hiding inside this castle because of her unholy reputation!" thought Jacob as he watched her hump grow. He wiped his eyes and all returned to normal, "I guess I'm just learning to adapt to a different kind of culture and lifestyle. Perhaps their thinking is weirdly contagious." Jacob forced himself to relax and smiled as if he forgave and was forgiven, "Good day Knyazhna

Zoryana! Come join me!"

"It is too early. Sun is damaging for the skin. It encourages age spots. I'll wait right here in the protective shadows," she gave him an unpleased glare, somewhat like a headmaster of a boarding school to an un-favored student.

"I see," said Jacob and then thought, "Like you should be afraid of age spots. I can't please you. Can I?"

Raising his glass in the air he loudly announced, "I'll come down."

While Jacob slowly walked toward Knyazhna, he progressively noticed differences in her appearance. Her hair almost fully covered the top of her skull and her eyes were much more open. There was enormous development in her dentures, the empty space of her upper arch was filled with teeth and more shocking was the beginning growth of her lower teeth. "You look wonderful!" mumbled Jacob, hardly containing his shock, "So renewed, rested."

"I had the beauty sleep," old Knyazhna answered with lustful confidence and an oddly added sweetness of a smile.

Jacob sensed the opposing game between them and thought, "The anger that Knyazhna showed earlier was clear manipulation." He saw his own set point of view of her and what he perceived her view was of him. He cheered his glass to hers and gently kissed her semi-warm hand that, lucky for him, was covered by an elegant glove. Jacob forced away his memory of last night but everything in Knyazhna's behavior seemed to suggest its reality.

"Positive emotions stimulate a woman's body, remarkably. Of course, through her mind first," Knyazhna gave a moment for Jacob to digest her statement and the modification in her appearance.

"I am sure they do," still bending, Jacob noticed a big set of eyes gazing at him from the devilish corridor that led to the kitchen. "Positive emotions are blessings to anyone," he bowed and walked to his chair at the other end of the dining table. He sat down and immediately requested, "Would it be okay to ask for coffee?"

Exactly at this moment Bohdan walked in with coffee in a silver pot.

"Anything you wish," flashing her new teeth old Knyazhna winked at Jacob.

Pleased with Knyazhna's positive attitude, Jacob cheerfully lifted his eyebrow. He then directed his eyesight to the table and the served dish, which contained a boiled egg, a slice of cheese and a slice of sweet corn muffin, all of which were not on the table a few minutes ago. "That is so nice of you, Bohdan, to have it all ready for me."

"You are very welcome, sir," Bohdan replied while filling Jacob's mug with coffee, "I prepared a mug for your coffee like you are used to in your homeland." Most oddly, Bohdan stretched his mouth that ended in a near scowl, which was intended to be not less than a friendly smile.

"It is absolutely superb, appreciate the effort. I just love my morning stuff hot," replied Jacob.

"I do too," cheered Knyazhna with her raised mug of coffee.

Sipping his coffee in haste, Jacob burned his mouth but kept it well hidden. He grabbed a silver knife and began to knock on the boiled egg, "What time is the celebration set for?"

"Half an hour before midnight," Knyazhna answered without delay, "You will be provided with an event appropriate wardrobe," in a tiresome, regal way Her Majesty Knyazhna sighed while looking at Jacob's casual outfit. "At that formidable time, which I considered glorious, the dress code was the reputable social face of a woman and man. When the division between 'Haute Couture' and 'Ready to Wear' did not exist, clothes were made to measure by a dressmaker, who worked directly with a single client. Suits for men were done the same way. The tailor, you would call today, cannot even compare to a seamstress's hands of those days," Knyazhna said pointing at Jacob's poorly fitted clothes.

Jacob was expecting the berating disgrace of modern man's wear, but the moral lessons of old Knyazhna ended suddenly when she continued to pick at small bits on her plate.

The feast became more enjoyable with the silence. To appease his appetite, Jacob avoided contact with Knyazhna's face in case she began her multi-meaning questions or her nutty suggestions that revolted him. She remained quiet. Jacob ate heartily. First, he finished the plate that was prepared for him, gulped down two cups of coffee then he moved to the remnants of an extremely delicious cold bird. He followed it by grabbing a few pieces of fruit then kicked back in his chair, letting his body slide down.

"That's a healthy boy, although perhaps with terrible manners," Knyazhna commented through labored breathing as the fleshy protuberance on her back moved up and down.

"Here it comes," Jacob opened one eye and caught the usual stare of old Knyazhna, but he was too satisfied for nonsense to ruin his contentment.

"I am pretty healthy. Thanks," he answered smoothly.

"That pleases me," she replied.

"Is it customary in this area for such late gatherings?" inquired Jacob to interrupt the old lady's sexual peeping from her cataract fish-like eye.

"It is."

"What will you be doing before that? Your

writings?" guessed Jacob, trying to be polite.

"Most likely," with effort, Knyazhna lifted the glass with her red drink and drank it.

"What should I do? Should I walk around? See the outside? That sounds like a good idea to me!" he answered himself in the same loud uplifting tone.

Knyazhna breathed so heavily that it looked like her hump was growing. "Perhaps, it will be something new for you," her words came out in a whisper.

A small ray of late daylight peeked through joining clouds into the window. Knyazhna Zoryana covered her face and began making loud moaning noises. The noise physically disturbed Jacob.

Bohdan expediently drew the curtains together and then helped the trembling old Knyazhna off her chair, "Your Majesty, you should have not risen so early. The daylight might exhaust you."

"Are you okay, Ladyship?" Jacob asked with whole-hearted worry then turned to Bohdan, "Is she ill? Is that some kind of..."

Knyazhna fragilely interrupted, "Ahh, we will meet again tonight." With Bohdan's help, she moved along the table reaching Jacob and very softly touched his hand, "It is very kind of you to genuinely care about me. I can tell."

"It is only natural for a human heart to be caring,"

sincerely answered Jacob.

"It is?" Knyazhna questioned, looking straight at Jacob.

He saw her single healthy eye filled with blackness turning into an endless black hole. Jacob felt chills all over his body and nodded in agreement. Bohdan and Knyazhna walked away. Hardly standing on his feeble legs as if under some kind of spell, Jacob sipped his drink and stepped toward the corridor leading to the entrance way.

The corridor remained as Jacob remembered it, like an underpass of night without a candle or a trace of light. He steadied his walk with his hands against the walls. A sudden smell, reminding him of a mushroom plantation, hit his nostrils. That, in combination with the darkness, made him feel slightly nauseous. Jacob finally found the heavy entrance door and pushed it open. The outside overcast sky almost blinded him, that surprise forced Jacob into an abrupt intake of breath; the free air traveled rapidly into his organs restoring his strength.

CHAPTER 8

THERE IS NOTHING OUTSIDE

EUROPEAN CASTLE, COURTYARD – LATE DAY

Full of excitement to inhale and exhale the outdoor freshness, Jacob stepped down the stairs onto the courtyard.

With his sobering mind, he acknowledged his revitalized energy, which awoke in him short-term gratefulness for his healthy physical attributes that he always took for granted. The outside, illogically provided him with a sheltered sense of safety. Yet the air itself seemed to be in some kind of unrealistic static state of preserved peace.

"I am sure there is a simple explanation for my disarray," he self-rationalized, "I was exhausted, a great deal overwhelmed with all the new impressions, and plus I ate excessively and drank way too much."

In a brief moment, all around seemed to him to be normal. "I don't know. Maybe all of this is not so bad? Different, but where else will I get paid so well for such adventures. The old Lady sometimes acts irrational, maybe over the top, but what can you expect at that age? I have never had to deal with that kind of old person before. And how old is she? Too old. Again, what I thought happened in my bedroom, was just an overwhelming impression, a nightmare, that's all," Jacob summed it up with an unfamiliar to him, analytical mind.

A light wind blew at his face, and, for the first time in his life, he regarded the basic things of nature as a miracle. There he yelled upbeat, "I never felt this before! How is it that I never knew this before! To be alive is good!"

"It is, though most don't think of it while being alive," the familiar voice of Bohdan joined the moment, "Relating to nature's elements; to earth, water, air, fire, or the emotions; love, hate, lust, sacrifice and to any of the faculties; as sight, hearing, the touch of caressing wind, or taste and smell, by which the alive perceive stimuli originating from outside or inside the body. All of these important senses for us are uncompounded, just beautifully elemental." Jacob turned and saw a strong and temporary emotional Bohdan behind him who enviously added, "I envy you."

"Why? Aren't you alive as me?" Jacob said with a little sarcasm. "Enjoy it as well!" There he started to break out in a slight sweat from Bohdan's long stare.

"Envy of your youth, sir," finally Bohdan cracked the tension.

"I guess it is a blessing," Jacob answered.

"You should return inside the house sir. Soon. The weather may change any minute."

Jacob looked away and pointed to the gate, "I was planning to walk outside the castle." Hearing no response, Jacob turned back around and saw no one behind him. Getting used to surprise disappearances, Jacob rushed to the gate and pushed it open.

As the heavy grand gate cracked open, Jacob saw nothing but a thick fog that made it impossible to see a foot in front of him.

Bohdan's voice whispered into Jacob's ear, "There is nothing beyond the gate."

Realizing that there was still no one around, Jacob took it for another trick of the castle's occupants, "Don't be ridiculous. Of course there is," he said to no one and made a step forward through the semi-opened gate. Almost falling he caught himself on the gate's frame.

"Am I ridiculous or are you?" Bohdan's voice teased in Jacob's ear once again. Jacob twirled around to find the stoic servant standing nearby with a big smile. The weird part was not Bohdan's reappearance but rather his cheerfulness.

"What the hell?" asked Jacob. He backed up inside the courtyard and picked up a two-meter long stick. Again failing to see Bohdan, he walked back to the gate and stopped before crossing. He poked ahead with the stick, which disappeared into the fog, and pushed it lower and lower, as it seemingly dissolved into a smoky nothingness. Finally, he let go of the stick and only the echo of its landing was heard far below. Jacob stepped back in panic.

A sudden wind chased the clouds, turning them into dirty purple. Then lightning struck, splitting the sky into shattered pieces, like a plate that had been dropped. It was followed by a rattling thunder trailing into the wobbling ground. The percussive shock awakened Jacob's survival senses.

Jacob ran through the courtyard back to the castle. He tried to open the door, but it was locked; he banged on it but the thunder was louder. He shouted, "Hey! Let me in! Hey! Hey! Open up! Hey, Bohdan!" He was distracted by a thin high-pitched sound that competed with his screaming. He looked down and saw dozens and dozens of rats. Their squeaking became unreal, louder than thunder, "God damn, Bohdan, let me in!"

Finally, Bohdan's figure appeared in a small

window. "Sir Jacob! Do you want your suitcases? I thought you wanted to leave?" Bohdan shouted down. The storm was progressing out of control.

"No. No! I want to stay! Please open up!"

The door opened on its own. Jacob stepped back letting a thousand wet rats rush inside. Then himself, he hurried in and watched the panicking rats scurried into ground level cracks in the wall. A pleased-faced Bohdan joined him to gaze as the last refugee disappeared into a crack.

"Poor creatures. Their outside path has been blocked for a while from a previous natural disaster. In days like this, they come in through here to hide from predators. The rain makes them weak," Bohdan's voice carried in a soft sentimental tone.

Jacob asked nothing else while the word 'predator' looped in his ear.

Holding a single candle, Bohdan offered, "Let me walk you to your room, sir."

CHAPTER 9

ODD CELEBRATING THE ODD

EUROPEAN CASTLE, BEDROOM – EVENING

Wrapped in a pumpkin plaid throw with gold twisted fringes at the edge, Jacob looked through the window at the windy rainstorm. The sound of screaming rats still resonated in his ears although a little less. He felt safe watching Bohdan who was arranging the fire. Jacob sat in the rocking chair and began to meditate on the flame while it consumed branches, transforming them into ashes. In the short time of staying within the castle walls he had developed a taste for this kind of warmth and recalled nothing of California's year round heat. "How soon we adapt to seclusion," he thought.

"Sir Jacob, the fireplace is working perfectly. I will make some tea for you. Do you wish anything else, sir?" Bohdan bowed.

"Coffee would be better. Thanks, Bohdan," he replied with appreciation, "Wait what is this throw made of? It holds the heat incredibly?"

"Hand-loomed wool, sir. And of course gold thread."

As soon as Bohdan exited, Jacob's calmness switched to anxious insecurity and he began to argue in his mind, "This is all ridiculous. I must, I must leave! First thing tomorrow I will be out of here!" He dashed to his bed and buried his face in a pillow.

A lack of oxygen forced Jacob to lift his head from the pillow. Bohdan was already awaiting near the bed with the coffee, he placed the tray on the night table and walked away. Listening to the crackling of the fireplace, Jacob sipped his coffee in contemplation, "This is definitely strange. I don't think I've ever spoken that much to myself until now. Is this abnormal? What else do you do with the absence of connection to the outer world? I guess if you're stuck on an island alone, you'd talk to yourself." Jacob placed the empty cup on the night table and spread his body out over the four-post bed, "Oh damn. It's comfy." He then scrunched up into a fetal position.

EUROPEAN CASTLE, BEDROOM - NIGHT

Whether it was a solid short nap or a long comatose restful sleep, it was impossible to determine unless Jacob checked his watch before and after awakening. But he was too emotionally exhausted to consider tracing time. Sinking deeper into peacefulness, Jacob was strongly subjugated by an imageless sleep. A loud knock on the door startled him. With heart-beating anxiety, he watched the door open, it was Bohdan holding fine extravagant clothes. Jacob did not give a thought of who they belong to.

"You frightened me, Bohdan! Why did you knock so loud?" accusatively exclaimed Jacob with sweat coming out on his forehead.

"You are mistaken. I have learned of the sensitive nature of yours and knocked very gently, Sir Jacob," answered Bohdan politely. He walked to the closet and carefully put the garments away.

"The sound must have hit a nerve in my sleep and ...." Jacob did not finish his conclusion and instead swung his legs out of bed.

"Sir, here is warm water for you to freshen up before the celebratory night." Bohdan pointed to a table with a bowl of hot water and a towel. Jacob placed his hands in the water for a few long moments. It felt very pleasant. Then he splashed his face which allowed his frown to relax.

"Please hurry, sir. You are expected shortly," Bohdan reminded him from the doorway.

Jacob looked around then shouted, " Wait! Where are my jeans?"

"Ah, forgive me, sir," Bohdan explained patiently, "Your dress coat and your trousers are in the closet."

Suspecting sarcasm, Jacob rushed to the closet. "You must be kidding me," he replied as he studied the costume. "It's for a freaking carnival!"

"I am afraid not. It is absolutely mandatory for you to wear the provided clothes," advised Bohdan sternly. He then turned and shut the door on the way out.

It took a few more splashes of water on his face and full body stretches for Jacob to awaken his courage to go back to the colorful wardrobe. He took the clothes out of the closet and laid them on the bed. It was an eighteen century three-piece suit; a gentleman's frock; a long-tailed coat made of thin red wool in classic French style, embroidered with gold thread and lined with gold silk. Underneath the frock was a gold waistcoat with a red velvet design, glittered with fine transparent red crystals, also adorned with embroidered gold thread. And lastly, there were white breeches with gold and red trim, with fun details like its fly fastening belt, the original version of the zipper. Jacob stared at the suit for a long while. The style of the frock, in some way, reminded him of a standing frog or a lizard. The back side of it had knee length tails while the front ended not too far below the waist.

At first Jacob resisted the idea of wearing the glittery clothing, but after looking closer, he began to run his fingers along the elaborate embroidery of the waistcoat and frock, becoming more familiar and friendlier to the fine art of haute couture. Toward the back of the closet he found ruffled white shirt and linen undergarments; an undershirt and eighteenth century drawers, the predecessor of underpants. Finally, he pulled out knee high violet suede boots with hand-embroidered gold crowns all over them.

EUROPEAN CASTLE, BALLROOM - NIGHT

It was becoming customary for Jacob to look down at the living room from a top floor inner balcony before walking downstairs. This night the chandeliers were linked by shimmery garlands and white paper bats hung from the castle ceiling; that made the view extra enchanting. Jacob was taken back by the adorned layout. The room carried a grandeur and unique aroma yet was tainted with a relic flair.

Down below, Bohdan sounded nostalgic and proud, "A very long time ago this hall was a ballroom, arranged in Royal splendor to welcome noble for social gatherings."

"Is it pumpkin or cinnamon or some Middle

Eastern oil, or all of that mixed together?" Jacob thought and wiggled his nose in the air trying to guess the scent.

"Nutmeg," Bohdan answered gladly.

Jacob deliberately paused at the top stair, posturing for approval of his look. Bohdan finished a final touch of the table's arrangement and now had time to accommodate the dear guest. He raised his hands and applauded. Jacob took the flattery in, bowed and confidently walked down the stairs.

"Am I too early?" Jacob greeted Bohdan with a sharp military salute.

"Not too early. Only a little early. Punctuality is a quality of Kings," Bohdan answered formally and very friendly offered him a choice of exquisite cigars from a wooden box with gold embellishments.

"All right, king! Did you see these buttons? I hope to keep them as a souvenir," Jacob twisted a button on his frock.

Bohdan's tone changed to one of a snobbish aristocrat, "The buttons are pure gold and approximately two hundred and fifty years old. They are valuable antiques, not a souvenir from a seaside shop, sir."

"Bummer! I really like them! Are you sure they're that old?"

Bohdan nodded with knowledgeable confidence.

"Well, I love the outfit," Jacob tilted his head closer to Bohdan's ear and whispered, "Except the boots, they are a bit girly, the color and crowns..."

"These are the original coronation boots of Gustav III of Sweden from the Royal Armory!"

"Bologna!" exclaimed Jacob. Noticing the reaction of Bohdan, he tried to speak more vigorously and placed the wrong end of a cigar between his lips. "Splendid then. I don't really know this Gustav dude, but if he was a king, that does it for me." Bohdan assisted him to reposition the cigar. "Appreciate it," Jacob held his chin up.

"Not at all," replied Bohdan and lit their guest's cigar with a large match, "Looking irresistibly dashing, sir Jacob."

"Flattered, Bohdan, but I am trying to keep on a traditional road," spoke Jacob half sarcastically.

"Traditional in your understanding, sir? I assume that would be vintage or antique," Bohdan seemingly teased him.

"Sorry man, perhaps this doesn't happen in your region? You know, when one man likes another man?"

Bohdan's face was blank for a few seconds, then he answered, "Brothers?"

"Sort of. Forget it man, it was a joke," Jacob regretted starting the subject.

"So was mine," Bohdan answered dryly. "Good luck with trying the traditional way, sir," walking away, Bohdan unexpectedly burst out in laughter, "Good luck!"

Knyazhna Zoryana appeared in the doorway of a dark corridor, wearing a black ball gown and a small hairpiece that decorated her nearly bald skull.

"Good evening, Knyazhna," Jacob inhaled the smoke from his cigar.

"Ladyship or Your Majesty, would be more suitable," approaching form behind, Bohdan whispered to Jacob.

"Sure. Thanks," Jacob coughed a few times, "Forgive me, Your Majesty, Knyazhna! I'll do my best to learn. We Americans aren't really into that, royalty and titles, but I guess its prestigious in Europe. You look very chic."

"That wasn't a compliment worthy of royalty, but he tried at least," thought Knyazhna.

Bohdan poured three glasses of wine from the bottle he brought. They all drank.

"I don't see the crowd. Where is everyone?" asked Jacob but no one answered. He persisted, "People, guests?" Bohdan and Knyazhna looked at each other.

"I mentioned nothing of a crowd. I only announced the celebration," Knyazhna replied.

Hoping for civilized entertainment and human communication, Jacob had to hold his breath to control his disillusionment. "Well then," he suspected deceit in her answer, so he walked to his seat.

"Let us dine first," ordered Knyazhna and walked to her chair without support.

When she turned, Jacob noticed her hump was less visible than before and said, "If I had a castle like this, I would have it filled with people, parties, all kinds of events. I would invite movie stars, producers..." At first Jacob was speaking his wishes and then he became lost in his imagination. A few moments passed and he returned from his fantasy to find both Bohdan and Knyazhna staring at him. They started to dine.

"If you behave as I wish," Knyazhna delivered to Jacob from across the table, sounding strong, "You might have this castle for yourself."

Jacob jumped up in his chair like a happy young puppy, "Really, that would be cool! This castle would be full of energetic people, full of life!"

Bohdan's stoic voice interfered with Jacob's moment, "That would be splendid."

"Splendid, what? Energetic people!?" Jacob asked.

"Instead of cool, I would use splendid," Bohdan corrected him back.

"Yeah, whatever you say in your medieval language," agreed Jacob.

"I see nothing wrong with either energetic or full of life," added Knyazhna happily.

Jacob joined their seemingly blissful mood and smiled inwardly all through dinner, imagining that he owned this castle. About ten minutes into the quiet banquet, an overhasty fright entered his mind, "What exactly will I have to do to earn this castle?" Once again catching the penetrating stare of Knyazhna he almost vomited. To hide his anxiety he slurped from the wine glass.

Old Knyazhna saw all of Jacob's fears and felt like triggering them to test his strength, "You might need to share your soul, tasting the depth of darkness where I reside. Expose your flesh to let me feel your organs beating against your warm skin." Knyazhna pulled some skin off of a piece of duck.

Jacob swallowed in pain as if his own skin was being pulled off. From a distance valley, loud and sad wolves' howls echoed and traveled through the castle. Knyazhna seemed to be adoring the noise.

Knyazhna gazed to the window and spoke,

"Sweet weeping yowl, a lullaby for the newly perished and most penetrating time reminder to the soul of the alive. Such sound does not travel within the veins, full of heated blood, but echoes and resonates in lonely bones. And bones belong to living and to dead, melodic instrument to the unseen."

Knyazhna finished her speech with a pulsating effect in her voice, like a vibrato, produced in singing.

The howls suddenly stopped, and the silence became even more haunting for Jacob. He had learned for now that any talking is helpful to break any harsh consequence, so he began, "Majesty, Knyazhna," he wiped his mouth with a napkin, and an idea struck him, "Would you like to dance, Your Majesty? I can sing a little to accompany the ball."

Jacob walked toward Knyazhna but passed her continuing into the corridor. He very precisely cleansed his hands in the washing bowl, watching for her approval. After a slight nod from Knyazhna, he dried his hands and ended up at her chair. He bowed as a gentleman would and offered her his hand. Knyazhna looked pleased with Jacob's effort to absorb her demands and gave him her hand. Jacob escorted her to the center of the room and began his singing. They moved very slowly and the old Knyazhna Zoryana's face glowed with gladness.

"This castle used to hold the most glorious balls. I was still beautiful then, I was princes Zoryana," old Knyazhna's eyes sparkled with sadness. She let herself be led by youth, who mumbled a nice allegro tempo rhythm to their moves. She enjoyed it tremendously, yet frazzled from the triggered ruins of her forgotten memories and perhaps more so from the physical movement of dancing, Knyazhna pointed to the chairs near the fireplace, "Please, I need some rest."

Fancying himself a bit of warmth, Jacob eagerly escorted Knyazhna toward the fireplace. He actually felt a pinch of sympathy and care for the old lady. After a few minutes watching the flame and saying nothing to each other, Jacob made an effort to generate a question in his head, but had trouble in concentrating from all the wine he had drank. He opened his mouth a few times attempting to speak, but each time Knyazhna almost fell into his mouth with her piercing attention and he could not do it.

Finally, after exercising his jaw and lips a few more times, Jacob spat out the first part of a question, "May I ask?" Knyazhna gestured for him to go ahead. Jacob asked while stretching his neck side to side, "Why don't you have any friends?"

Knyazhna was pleased that in the seemingly shallow mind of young Jacob rose any interest. Her Majesty Knyazhna spoke calmly,

"Friendship can easily be rejected when you are unable to afford

meaningless things. Yet, you may eventually find yourself at the ultimate destination where you need no one because you can afford everything. Even to hire a young vibrant body like you."

Her momentary pause seemed a lifetime to Jacob. He waited for something: a conclusion, advice, a proposal.

"Look at me," ancient Knyazhna implored as she looked down at her old hands then took off her hair piece, to expose her ill head, "Who would want to be my friend now, unless I pay them?"

Jacob felt incredibly guilty knowing that he was one of those people who would not do anything for an old person without reimbursement. This self-realization resounded in his mind, "I am one of those profit motivated hypocrite free-spirited phonies. Even if she was a distant relative of mine, I would not stay long without some kind of reward. I wonder if I would have ever even visited her, if not for excessive payment? What if she lived in a tiny house with no servants and I had to clean and cook for her?" He felt sincerely embarrassed. Wanting to cheer up the old sad woman, he directed his inquiry into Knyazhna's beautiful past, "What about those times when you held, I would imagine, magnificent balls? Many of the invited must have been your close friends?" He hoped for a positive response.

Knyazhna squinted her eyes and answered sharply, as would businessman riposte to deals without compromises. "Those gatherings had a different purpose," she paused, "To feed the flesh."

Jacob did not exactly understand what she meant but interpreted her last phrase to be a mingling of couples with intention of getting to know each other better.

Suddenly, Bohdan reappeared and handed Her Majesty Knyazhna the manuscript. She inhaled and exhaled with her abdomen and the protuberant on her back moved up and down. Finally Knyazhna said, "And to select the 'Chosen'." Then she pushed the manuscript toward Jacob. Her hands shook as if instead of paper pages she was pushing thick plates made of gold.

Jacob was sorry for his arrogance toward the helpless old women. He watched her and swore to be kinder, "What does she have to look forward to? These scribbles are probably the only thin thread tying her to this world."

Knyazhna wished but could not disclose to anyone that for her these pages were the weight of gold, in the value of memory and in the mass of hurt. The mass so great that could crash through the earth's crust, as if it was breaking the planet's outermost rock layer, like the shell of an egg.

Old Knyazhna stroked the corner of her manuscript and said,

"As we leave our creation after we are gone, we are truly not gone. If you produced a child who remembers you, or mastered a painting that looks out with eyes of comprehension onto an on looking stranger, or your sole-picked composed words, kept read with lips of the alive, repeated into the breathable air, that is what makes your own soul swirl on this earth or other, long after your body is not."

Still leaning toward the pages, she weakly cleared her throat. Her tongue circled over her dried lips, then she pulled herself back into the chair, and respired, "Back then, the age of splendor and harmony, refined elegance and opulent ornamentation, it was fashionable for the elite to play social games. Our court played distinct games of purpose..." Mumbling, Knyazhna lost herself in memory, or, perhaps she had no intention to share all of her secret treasures at once. She stopped talking.

Watching the silent Knyazhna, Jacob seemed to see her speaking fast and unclear. That uneasy sensation lasted for almost a minute. He felt a tingling on the back of his neck.

Knyazhna continued in full voice as if she had not interrupted her out-loud speaking, "Well hopefully you have a vivid imagination as the young should have and with the reading, you may see the grand magnificence of the times when I was fresh as a blossom." She stretched her smile for the purpose of smiling, and then her mood changed to one of sulking. With pain displayed on her face, she weightily moved her jaw.

Jacob's imagination began to fill in a scene, envisioning a large group of people holding hands. They circled in some kind of ritual or perhaps a traditional Eastern European dance of celebration. But it must have been a 'Mourning Celebration' as the dancers' faces showed great sadness. He saw nothing like what Knyazhna described of a social elite game of "Chosen." The dance in Jacob's visualization, became faster and faster, and he felt dizzy as if he was directly involved in it.

Knyazhna waved to Bohdan to refill Jacob's goblet. Jacob could hardly lift his drink but drank it with the thirst of a desert wanderer. Trying to regain clarity of mind, he stood up. Knyazhna lustfully smiled at Jacob's very tight pants and commented, "If you should be present at the ball, you need to practice to wear those kind of breeches."

Resigned to his fate and the current moment, Jacob took the manuscript and prepared to read.

CHAPTER 10

GLORIOUS BALL OF THE PAST

EUROPEAN CASTLE, MAIN HALL, GLORIOUS BALL - FLASHBACK - NIGHT

Memories of a glorious ball flashed and old Knyazhna was not old anymore. She was the young Princess Zoryana in a red velvet dress and striking mask of precious stones.

Senior Stewards of the Keep ushered in the exalted guests to pay their respect with deep bows to the young Majesty Knyazhna Zoryana who welcomed them from the balcony above. The exquisitely well-dressed guests, gentleman in frocks and ladies in long gowns of royal blue, emerald green, blood red velvet and sparkling ornamental icy hued brocades, were in a virtuous playful mode. Adorned and armed with arcane gilded silver and gold, the castle's opulence was projected into its interior by the imperishable might of the presence of liveliness.

Three Red Judges emerged on the top floor balcony. They all appeared to be the same height with a mature thin build. They wore black velvet frock coats with immaculate long tails and blood-red masks of unknown beasts. Crowned with Egyptian guardian cat ears, each mask was ornamented with owl-feathers around the eyes and had a short eagle beak with human nostrils on the sides. By their upright postures and sharp supervising look, the Judges resembled guard dogs ready to locate enemies.

Hiding half of her face under a mask worth a king's ransom, young Knyazhna Zoryana was proudly exposing the youth of her luscious lively lips, sky blue eyes, young neck and her thin yet full of strength shoulders. An enormous thirteen carat, round cut, vivid blue Ceylon sapphire broach on her dress was a direct connection to her identity and the vigilance toward the passage of unauthorized deeds.

Knyazhna Zoryana's voice floated above,

"I preferred emeralds, the stone of vitality! Yet, the Ceylon sapphire had meaning, a significant meaning in my life. This vivid blue gemstone's unique attribute is that it gives off thirteen percent violet as a secondary hue. I loved that drop of violet, the

end of the visible spectrum of light, between blue and invisible ultraviolet. It was that border where I left one side of the visible ordinary formula of life known to all, and transitioned myself to the distinct hues of the extraordinary human, those of Royal Blood, known to all yet never visible in commonplace."

A million times tormentedly tempted, Knyazhna wanted to share the story of obtaining that broach. It was her pride of prides, it was her birth, it was her ability to present the esoteric gift to the next extraordinary delivery. Though her lips were sealed, her voice hovered within the monumental walls sounding distant. Patrolling the guests, Knyazhna Zoryana and the Judges were fortifying the glamour of the future, as the past interlaced with the present, and the pages of the manuscript were turning and spoken.

"In the not so distant past, a proper high society rule was that, to dance or even to speak at a court ball, the guests must be introduced by a third party. Mine, 'The Knyazhna Zoryana's Ball' was famous for the breaking of those rules and everyone dreamed of being there. Two distinctions attracted the wealthy and

the poorer nobles: The Dance of Silence with strangers and 'Excerptus' the game of captivating words with unrevealed partners. The wealthy high-bidders craved excitement. And the poor nobles, whose funds barely exceeded their need, dreamed of the opportunity to marry into greater wealth."

A happily sounding bell in the hand of the Head Steward announced the start of the ball. All the faces of the anticipating guests raised their gaze for Knyazhna Zoryana's permission. The precisely paired strangers awaited direction of the stewards for their turn to enter onto the dance floor.

"The Ball began with The Dance of Silence. Partners were assigned by order of arrival. Couples or groups of arriving guests were divided and given a masked stranger. Only movement and laughter were allowed."

The lasting 'Silent Dances' were truly harmoniously marvelous. Petals and shimmering confetti were falling from the balcony onto the dancing couples. Everyone was overly excited, even if they were not paired with their desired partner, because the time of the game was becoming closer.

The blissfully sounding 'Intermission Bell' gave ease to the dancers' feet and hosted festivity treats. A banquet of refreshments and food was announced open.

Uplifted from the over stimulating entertainment, the hungry and thirsty guests rushed to the heavenly platters of delicacies.

"The interlude gave rest and a chance to feast, yet still in wordless motion. Dashing heightened attraction by imagination, burst in everyone's mind: Who had been singled out? What was their age, name and status in society?"

Unsuitably excited with their new secret acquaintances, excess consumption of rich cuisine and fabulous refreshments, the guests and members of the court began to lose their posh and pompous postures. However, even the splendor of the regal event could hardly compare to the glowing radiance of Knyazhna Zoryana's youthfulness.

The bell rang again but this time in an alerting tone! Young Knyazhna stood on the balcony in her red dress, flanked by the Red Judges.

"Excerptus - the Game of Chosen, would immediately begin. The contestants would hastily rush to

introduce themselves, without giving away their names, nor court status. Self-Introduction was a clear infraction of the formal traditions of the time, yet it was not breaking the rules of the game. The invitees' exceptional excitement was, in fact, the opportunity to be accepted into high society even if they were from outside the court."

The eldest Judge, distinguished by an extra ribbon over his coat and a gold badge, spoke down. He explained the game to the newcomers.

"The rules are simple. Contestants must promptly exchange words with each other, connecting them into a simple sentence. Those who changed the most partners will be rewarded with fabulous prizes, gold and other greater treasures."

At that moment, an owl flew over the guests and sat on Young Knyazhna's shoulder pinning everyone's attention to her. Knyazhna announced,

"Yet, when the game is interrupted, all must become motionless. The luckiest captured in

the most curious static pose of their last movement will be proclaimed the Chosen, known in Great Latin as, Excerptus!"

Having fed their digestive needs and now each carrying a glass of exquisite indulgence, the contestants assimilated into the rhythm of the bizarre, seemingly simple game. It was easy for the members, but, more so, its main design had to be as easy for the newcomers. All the players had to do was say words to each other, connecting them into a sentence of at least three words.

The game was played quickly in order to change more partners for socializing and a better chance to win the remarkable prizes. The elegant guests-contestants exchanged few words then moved to the next partner with apparent joy and inquisitiveness. Some of the players were leaving their partners with laughter, a few with disappointment and many with the hope to make the round as fast as possible to rejoin their favorite companions again. In some occasions it was difficult to say goodbye to a favorable partner.

The game of "Chosen" was in full force. The masked Red Judges and young Majesty Zoryana viewed the connecting links and witnessed the cheats from the balcony above. The honorable Judges were there not to serve the whims of their guests but to regulate the sway and flow, for a purpose higher than social prestige. Their duty required them to discover a worthy candidate to become the Chosen, the Excerptus.

Bridging with the present, the sound of rustling pages and Jacob's monotone reading of the manuscript intruded into Knyazhna's enchanted glory of the past.

Knyazhna turned her eyes to Jacob as he began,

"Excerptus, Child of Nosferatu.

The entrance of The Preeminent Nosferatu into the mortal world with the capability of infinite life was denied nature's most crucial demand for the continuity of a species, the vitality of reproduction. Therefore, a way had to be found to breed the next vampire,

Signed Knyazhna Zoryana."

Seemingly offhand with the game's ease of improvisation, determined gamblers began to force their company onto new partners, especially if they were newcomers.

"A garden-fresh young lady entered the premises and gasped, not from the deficiency of oxygen, but to

inhale the opulence into her pristine throat, to steal a drop of it. Nevertheless, she could not see the motive of the gentlemen watching her, wishing to grasp her breath, to drain her priceless purity."

Six men encircled the noticeably inexperienced young girl. Her face absolutely glowed with the first blossom of adulthood and the adoration of wealth. Yet, she was still a child in her lips, her eyes, and her skin, which was obviously virgin to any cover up make up as well as her pupils to romance. How she found her way into the castle was unknown, no one truly cared about that detail, only that her fresh presence was now in front of them. She was not even bait; she was a moist caught fish on a plate ready to consume. To be eaten raw as is.

"At the game, there were plenty of young ladies that were called 'Ripes', as in ripe fruit. They were ready to be taken and ready to give every inch of their body as well as their will. 'Ripes' were burning with desire. They were producing, releasing and splashing their chemical pheromones into the environment as animals do, strongly affecting their and others physiological behavior,"

the voice of old Knyazhna described.

Yearning women in their animalistic reproductive cycles, like lions or panthers were circling around, ready to pounce on anyone who was not careful enough to suppress their sensual interest. In the dark corridors, ladies' skirts were lifted, the gentlemen's trousers were unfastened, and the windows were opened to cool the overheated air. Those were mostly atmosphere guests.

"The court members could have that flesh anytime, yet their urge was taken with the essential prize, the innocent young girl who would be named Daisy. The masked Red Judges with the top of their heads wreathed by Egyptian cat ears, definitely craved to watch their mouse being toyed with a little longer. Each of the handsome devils surrounding the mouse, the moist fish, were desperately trying to become her partner, to speak to her, to look straight at her, to exchange sensual breaths with simple words. What an extravaganza! For the men it was a manifestly sexual game rather than social communication. They would care not at the least what word

*she would say, but they would try to
engage a few more words to continue
the sentence, to prolong their time of
intimate interaction."*

"This is our Daisy. We will refer to her as Daisy," Knyazhna sanctioned while watching the game from her bird's eye view. The Red Judges approved and agreed.

Standing near by on the balcony, Ladies of the court peered down at the male newcomers. Young Knyazhna Zoryana focused her gaze toward them and continued, "We should not be unfair to men, accusing only them of their lustful nature.

*'Here under the roof of this great
castle with its centuries old stone
walls, gathered mature Ladies of the
Court who picked their victims of
pleasure. Contrary to the men, who
followed their prey in a very intimate
proximity, the ladies were watching
their candidates from a distance'."*

The Court females were singling out the amateur newcomer males, who desired it all; the body, the wealth, the admiration, something they would not obtain from equal age girls. The harvest of the freshman would be in the mature Ladies' possession sooner than the girls being chased by the accomplished Men of the Court.

A few giant steps away from Knyazhna Zoryana on the balcony, another lasting game was in progress with a group of only two. A well-preserved seasoned lady, in a sequenced silver dress, The Silver Goddess of Lust, had it all for her desires to be fulfilled. She revealed the smooth skin of her leg in front of a very 'firm' young man, who by all accounts was a stallion among horses. Alike a stallion, a non-castrated male horse who had just entered its adulthood, the fresh gentleman's excitement was strongly exposed in his pants and his cravings were agile enough to take off without any wasted movement of his hoof. The heightened anatomy enabled such species to respond to their animalistic desires and use their speed to escape any predator, in this case the Silver Goddess. However, this one's nature was at the cycle of responding to the healthy temperament of 'hot blood' focusing on furthering his breed.

Looking at him, Knyazhna Zoryana was pleased, "This boy is a wild spirit. We must name him Mustang."

"Mustang it is," the Red Judges agreed.

Sweet Daisy was struggling with her first act of rejection. She stood in the center of a surrounding group of corrupt men. She did not see their deceitful strategy, but she knew she must pick one them for the game. With closed eyes, Daisy spun around, stopped and pointed at a randomly chosen partner.

"Wildcat," she started.

"Snuck," answered her first picked partner.

"In," Daisy added.

"The house," the first man finished the sentence.

Daisy turned and challenged the next partner with the same word, "Wildcat."

"Fell," he suggested.

"In milk," she finished.

Another young man who was too impatient for being her next game partner intruded and added, "Cat became."

Daisy laughed, "A wet pet."

Obviously, the game did not intend to spotlight knowledge or literary skill. It was designed for fast fun, for leveling uneven degrees of intelligence. It was created to discard arrogance and competition to enable socializing that breached the borders and barriers of nobility and distant aristocratic posh behavior.

The kind-hearted Daisy wished for even a stray cat in a made up story to have a good fate. Everyone in the enclosed group was thrilled by her sweet character. However, the game had to continue and Daisy had to move on, as per the rules, to the next company. The participants were obviously not strict followers of the rules of grammar, but visually they followed the requirement of the game and periodically moved on to a next partner.

The Silver Goddess continued to be in the middle of a long sentence with her young eager Mustang. Regardless of his tight pants exposing his prowess as a virile stud, Mustang behaved as a gentleman. He did not force his erotic might onto her until The Silver Goddess tore her sequined dress and opened it up on one side. She looked down at his white pants and said, "Stone."

Mustang added, "Always is."

"Harsh," The Silver Goddess said and added, "Comma."

"Stone," proudly posing Mustang exclaimed.

"Is heavy," she exhaled.

"Must we..."

"Be buried beneath?" The Silver Goddess brushed against his stone shaft and pulled his arm to follow her. The Goddess and Mustang rushed toward a distant wing of the castle where their impatient vision was already directed and where their sentence would most positively end.

For a moment, the blood-Red masked Judges watched the couple leave and then returned their attention back to the ballroom. The Red Judges never left the second floor balcony like hawks guarding their nest; protecting their future. They surveyed the moves and engagements of the guests, analyzing the finale of the contestants' conversations. They carefully pondered for the right moment to interrupt the vivacity for their monumental decision.

For the honorable court members, it was not just an excessive indulgence of their social life, it was devotion to their duty to the court to elect the 'Chosen, Excerptus'.

As every wolf was repeatedly examining the little lamb Daisy, someone resembling an earlier version of Bohdan, watched the wolves.

Conversationally engaged contestants protracted their sentences longer and longer. They gesticulated with their shoulders and hips, replenished their drinks too many times and yet they were still connecting words in their determined play.

"The sound of the bell from the graveyard traveled directly into the ballroom. It reminded everyone of the approaching inevitable selection. The time when the game must be interrupted, when the best bait, caught in the grandest pose, would be carried motionlessly to the 'Room of Eternity' and proclaimed, 'The Chosen, The Excerptus'."

For the newcomers this was the most ultimate excitement. They knew nothing of what was coming. They expected the most unexpected and their biography would change forever if 'Chosen'.

Daisy made quite a few rounds and ended up near the fireplace where she had started. She seemed quite exhausted and even looked around to hide for a short rest. As she leaned her fresh shoulder against the wall beside the fireplace, the voice of a mature gentleman, startled Daisy.

"Iskus Itel," the gentleman announced his name, shamelessly breaking the rules of the game. Iskus Itel was not only seasoned in appearance by his salt and pepper facial hair, with groomed beard beginning at his temples and connected to his mustache, he conveyed the impression of a wise man. His style had a demeanor of power and lust; known to the perceptive to be a dangerous combination. He could have been a leader of Court or a camouflaged Red Judge.

Daisy looked lost, lost in her partner's imposing presence or perhaps in her intuition of something completely unseen that was about to happen. None of us ever believed that something horrific would ever happen to us, but most of us have had an experience of the feeling that it might. And when it happened we finally acknowledged it. But it was too late.

Iskus Itel read every thought of the young naive youth, "Please don't be alarmed by the unfamiliar, dear Daisy."

"But my name is not Daisy, Sir Iskus," she answered with great politeness.

"It is now. It was voted by all, even by the Blood Judges," Iskus Itel pointed up to the balcony where the red-masked Judges bowed to Daisy. She bowed in reverence in return. Iskus Itel gazed directly at her, "The freshness you carry is as rare as a rainbow in the dark. Your name must reflect the power over whom you wish to conquer. And that is your power. A pure naivety, so rare as the first inhaled bloom of spring," Iskus Itel smiled fatherly, "Naivety, unaffected simplicity of nature, the absence of artificiality. The lack of experience and judgment that near-sighted ignorance we will refer to as un-sophistication, that is in fact, the most powerful charm of innocence." Stepping closer to Daisy, who could not process all that had been said to her, he continued, "My name, must only be pronounced all at once, Iskus Itel. In the old Eastern European tongue, it means, 'The man who tempts', ISKUSITEL."

"As in the Temptation? The tempting of Jesus by the Devil as in Matthew?" Daisy spoke fast and then froze not knowing if it was appropriate to share her love of Bible study.

Iskus Itel burst out in laughter, "Ha, ha, ha, ha! I don't think I can recover a memory since I last laughed so joyously. Do you truly see me as a devil, my child, because I am older and a man?" in front of the word 'man' he emphasized an article 'A', which sounded to Daisy like 'Amen'.

Reflectively Daisy repeated, "Amen," and then corrected herself, "God bless you, sir. I meant nothing of that sort. It is my Christian study that I quoted," she said and appeared to feel terribly out of place.

"Bless you, sweet child," he petted her soft hair, "If I say 'Amen,' I should not be related to Satan. What do you think, dear Daisy?" Iskus Itel smiled so kindly that suddenly Daisy felt safe.

"Forgive me, sir. Is-kus Itel. I am not used to gatherings like these. I am more aquatinted to obedient worshiping churchgoers," Daisy's eyes sparkled and shy redness emerged on her cheeks.

"Worship is a mandatory in this house. Be at ease my obedient sweetness," Iskus Itel kissed her hand and pulled a large daisy flower from his inner pocket. It was fresh as if it had been just picked.

A sudden heat attacked everyone at once. The guests who had attended this event previously lifted their masks, took off their hats, unfastened their capes and delicate shoulder covers. In that instant, the thunder rattled and cold rain poured outside. No one screamed. No one was worried except Daisy. Returning from a long walk with his Silver Goddess, Mustang shivered. The flames of most of the candles died from a thunderous draft, yet, the flame in the fireplace became stronger. Servants closed all the windows at the same time and secured the handles with iron locks at all of the entrances. The attentive staff served special heated red wine which had a tint of spice and its aroma filled the room. The overwhelming jubilation gently subsided and gradually turned tranquil.

Now, the greatest worry of Daisy and Mustang was that they would not get a chance to win the grand prize, due to the subdued atmosphere that hardly would produce the perfect platform for a peculiar invigorating motion to occur. Daisy also saw nothing in her new partner, Iskus Itel, the old gentleman, that would spark a thrilling moment of action for a monumental pose.

Iskus Itel began their game, "Shadow."

"Shadow?" asked Daisy, "Excuse me?"

"Your turn dear Daisy, after my 'Shadow'," explained
Iskus Itel.

"Grew," almost automatically replied Daisy.

"From shallow depth," continued Iskus Itel.

"Into the deep," she said, plugging her fragility into Iskus Itel's seasoned grayness, which seemed to give her tranquility like a blessing by a priest.

"Dark hole," he then added, "Comma," and looked straight into the Daisy's baby blue eyes. A fright rushed over Daisy's little shoulders and she felt as if she was falling somewhere very deep. Her legs were losing strength.

"Where you lose," said Daisy weakly, describing her state but trying to go on toward the dreamingly illustrious victory of the game. She lifted her shoulders up to wake herself, "Comma."

"Your human breath," Iskus Itel suggested, closely leaning toward Daisy's innocent face. A butler caught her glass, while her eyes were disengaging their focus. Iskus Itel caught Daisy.

"Surrounded by the darkness of its walls," finished Daisy, who then disconnected from the reality of the event and time.

The Graveyard Bell resounded, penetrating the grand castle's walls. During Daisy's gradual fall into Iskus Itel's permanent embrace and Mustang's lower waist whiplash against the Silver Goddess's naked thigh, the Judges interrupted life in its form by suspending the game. Everyone froze. All their sensibilities were titillated, speculating in whispers over the captured situations of the other players.

Knyazhna's thick reading of the manuscript filled the spaces between the breaths of the present state.

"As a mother would nourish the child with her breast milk, the undead must feed the new human on the foul blood of the Nosferatu to

nourish them into the world of the chosen. Therefore, the Child of Nosferatu, adult or child is chosen not born to be EXCERPTUS with the eternal possibility of being present among the mortals. Excerptus is neither vitality nor dust.

Signed Knyazhna Zoryana."

Daisy and Mustang were 'Chosen'. Iskus Itel walked away with his unconscious naive little mouse, Daisy, in his arms. Mustang was lifted high in the air by six male court members, his head and arms hung down in a feigned insensible state. The chorus of members sang a farewell song, 'Ave, Hail of the Taking of the Chosen.' The non-court guests applauded the 'Chosen' for playing their parts well, in being physically 'disconnected'. Enjoying themselves while proudly completing their duties, the court members applauded the great finale. The unresponsive bodies of the 'Chosen' were carried up the stairway to the Room of Creation, the room of the 'Excerptus'.

EUROPEAN CASTLE LIVING ROOM – PRESENT - DAY

Backing up into the crease of her chair, old

Knyazhna moved away from Jacob. She resignedly gestured enough of the reading.

"Was I bad at reading?" Jacob assumed he was at fault.

Knyazhna shook her head in a negative way and leaned toward Jacob, gently touching his hand, "Very kind of you to ask, young man. You did well." Assuring him it was no fault of his, she continued, "What you think of your life now, one day will seem to you as something that never happened. Then you will question yourself,

> *'Am I old and imagining things, or was I part of that past that took the future for granted?'"*

old Knyazhna's naked eyelashes went wet from her tears.

"Is there really a possibility to live forever?" Jacob asked with seemingly genuine intent for information.

"Depending on... but definitely longer than you have knowledge of," replied Knyazhna casually.

"If I want to live forever, will I have to find a vampire and persuade him to let me be one of them?" Jacob was not sure himself if he was being serious by asking this.

"It is a crucial decision. You must not be hasty pronouncing such a wish out-loud, Jacob," Knyazhna leaned toward him and gently touched his face.

For the first time Jacob did not mind her touch. He felt he was changing somewhere inside, into a better, more concerned person. He began to realize that he was interested in other people's lives and opinions. More so, he seemed to discover incredible significance in life and all aspects of it, as well as curiosity in things that did not cross his attention in Hollywood, the town with its fast pace directed toward the end of ends.

"I don't want my life to end ever," insisted Jacob.

"You so much want to live forever, that you are ready to die for it?"

questioned old Knyazhna.

"Anytime! I promise, I'm sure," confirmed Jacob.

With a sly yet wise look old Knyazhna asked, "How can you be so sure?"

"Since my travel and after meeting you, I find myself curious in all sorts of things that, honestly, I have not even noticed before. In life itself with all of its complexities," Jacob spoke clearly. Knyazhna moaned and tried to get up from her chair. Jacob rushed to assist her.

"I must depart. My flesh is weak from all the exciting remembrance. It's getting anyway too late," Knyazhna slowly walked away toward the dark corridor.

"Are you going to be okay, Ladyship? Do you need assistance to your bedroom?" asked Jacob, still having no idea where her bedroom was.

"My bedroom is just around the corner. It's convenient for the elderly. Don't worry I will make it there. Thank you kindly," old Knyazhna walked away into the ceaseless darkness. Jacob grabbed a bottle of wine and ran, bounding up the stairs toward his bedroom.

From a dark corner of the inner balcony, Bohdan observed them both.

CHAPTER 11

GOOD NIGHT EXCERPTUS

EUROPEAN CASTLE, BEDROOM - NIGHT

Jacob entered his bedroom, locked the door and posed in front of the mirror. He loved what he saw, "I would look like this for a long, long time." Undressing, drinking and admiring himself in the mirror, Jacob finally lay in bed.

Both relaxed and thrilled at the same time, he cherished the thought of endless life. No matter how skeptical he was of any phantoms or extra-terrestrial phenomena, he could not stop thinking of immortality. Jacob finally fell asleep with the bottle in his hand and a big smile. Eventually, his grip loosened and the rest of the wine poured onto his white shirt and the white sheets.

EUROPEAN CASTLE, BEDROOM –
NIGHT (DREAM)

Although the door to Jacob's bedroom opened quietly, it woke him up anyway. He opened his eyes, but it took him a few moments to focus his drunken, sleepy vision. There she was, the beauty from the night before. The enchanting visitor giggled and ran back into the corridor. At first, Jacob struggled to get up, then he forced himself to his feet and rushed toward the open door. He stopped at the doorway and beckoned to the pretty guest to be quiet and to come back into the room. Instead, she walked backwards and dissipated into a what seemed to her a familiar darkness. Jacob returned to his room, looked the door behind him and walked back to his bed.

As he was climbing into bed, he felt a slight fresh breeze on his neck. He turned around and to his delight, he saw her, his happy angel, right before him. Dressed in her see-through long white gown, she extended her arms out to him. Jacob touched her cold hands, "It must be freezing out there. Come to bed." She gazed at him in a friendly way. "You don't understand my language?" Jacob half-asked half-stated, pulling her hand gently, "Come, it's warm." He helped her into his bed and covered her with a blanket. He sat in a chair near her, "If you understood me, I would ask you if you know how to become a vampire," Jacob spoke softly, while caressing her hand.

"Nosferatu," she whispered.

"Yes! Exactly! Nosferatu!" exclaimed Jacob. He examined her visually and saw nothing different from the multitude of beautiful women, that he had great experience in coming across. And yet, she reminded him of a beguiling spirit, a collective of characters from his favorite movies about young pretty ghosts full of tricks. Jacob felt an affinity toward her unlike any involvement he remembered, "Perhaps I want to see a young woman this way, as a spirit, with no attachment to any real female form. The real ones are needy, cunning or a burden. I myself am a free spirit and that would be ideal for me," Jacob felt pressure in his head from his overwhelming thinking. She touched his temple with her cold fingers. He let her cure his overstimulation.

"This is an impossible fantasy," he disputed his own wandering mind, while his fair visitor pointed at herself. "Yes I am thinking about you," Jacob replied at once. Her finger began to press hard on her lips then traveled to his neck. Jacob joked, "Are you a vampire?" She lifted her shoulders, smiled and shook her head up and down. He joked back, "Are you Nosferatu?"

She took his left hand and placed it on her chest pronouncing in Latin, "Excerptus. Excerptus. Excerptus."

Astounded and overwhelmed, Jacob was sure it was a misunderstanding due to a language barrier. Jacob made a movement with his hands like holding a baby. Then he pointed at her, "You are Chosen? You are Excerptus?" He stated it in a more serious questioning tone.

She lay on her back and pointed to her stomach, "Excerptus - Nosferatu." Then she touched her lips, sat up and touched his neck, "Nosferatu - Excerptus."

"You're kidding me right?" Jacob smirked, but she stared at him with demanding eyes.

She pointed at him then at her stomach and shouted in an echoing voice, "Excerptus! Excerptus! Excerptus!"

A chaotic fear overcame Jacob, "What if she is one of those vampires or those possessed?" He hopped up from the chair and backed away. She stood up on the bed. Jacob moved back. She took off her outer thin dress, leaving a completely see through under dress, looked at him and smiled. Jacob felt a sudden buzz running through his body to his head. He forced himself to return and took her hand, which wasn't so cold anymore. Her soft tingling touch raised Jacob's libido. He asked, "You want me to make you a child, then you can make me Child of Nosferatu?"

"Nosferatu. Nosferatu," she answered so sexually that Jacob was not completely sure what would happen, but he climbed into the bed anyway. She whispered something in his ear, kissed his neck and sat on top of him. Sounds of howling wolf-like animals filled the outside night. With a few intertwined movements of their hands, heads and her hair, the room darkened to a pitch black. The pleasures of flesh were timeless.

The rooster sang its day-breaking song and Excerptus fell on Jacob's chest and then rolled on her side laying next to him.

CHAPTER 12

WELCOME TO YOUR REALITY

EUROPEAN CASTLE, BEDROOM – MORNING

Jacob woke up robust and forceful, as if he had slept all through the night until mid-afternoon. He opened his eyes but saw no light peeking through the openings of the shutters, "Is it that early, or is it evening already?" He slowly started to dig into last night's events and recalled some with doubt, "Was it true? Could it only have been a dream?" He looked to his left and a shockwave ran though his head. There next to him, facing away, laid a female figure in white.

"Impossible, absolutely impossible. Is it her, Excer-ptus?" Jacob sputtered her name quietly in his mind. He strained his vision to see more in the darkness, to his horror, he found deep red stains all over the sheets. Timidly, he touched the woman's body in white but it was cold. His hand instinctively retreated. The fright of something abominable that could have happened last night paralyzed his ability to move. His mind cried, "No! Did I kill her? Why would I kill her? Did someone else kill her? Was it her?" he squeezed his head with his two hands, "God, what have I done? No! I had wine. It's only wine. I am sure of it." He touched her again. The cold body slightly trembled with breathing, "Excerptus. Was she just sleeping? I must hear if she is breathing," he leaned over. A wave of trepidation conquered his indescribable condition.

Hardly able to control himself from panicking, he got up to open the window, but it was locked from outside by the outer shutters. He looked in the mirror wrenching at his memory, "There must be some kind of explanation or am I still asleep?" Helplessly Jacob walked over to inspect the woman again. He covered his mouth with both hands to prevent screaming. "I am not sleeping and this is not Excerptus," he self-talked in his thoughts, staring at the decayed, century-old hunchback Knyazhna, who was sweetly sleeping in his bed.

He grabbed his jeans from under the bed and gathered one of his small suitcases. Unable to locate his t-shirt he took out a ruffled shirt, looked at old Knyazhna again and ran out of the room. "God I hope I did not have anything to do... ahahhh, with that hideous repugnant..! You can't even call it a woman, its embalmed left-overs of, ahhhhh!" he screamed inside his mind. With lightning-like speed, Jacob ran through the long corridor only in his underpants with ruffled shirt, jeans and suitcase in hand.

EUROPEAN CASTLE, LIVING ROOM – MORNING

Praying that he did not run into Bohdan, Jacob ran down the stairs into the living room still holding his clothes and small suitcase. Yet as soon as Jacob reached the bottom step, he noticed the ever snoopy Bohdan secretly observing from a dark kitchen corridor. Trying to disguise his intent, Jacob dropped his suitcase and proceeded to the dining area.

The table was set up meticulously. Bohdan casually revealed himself while pretending not to see anything wrong with Jacob who was almost naked, "Sir, would you like to wash your face?"

"Yeah. In fact I do!" Jacob irritatedly answered, dropped his clothes onto his chair and thoroughly washed his face, hands and chest with lavender soap.

Bohdan assisted him with a fresh water rinse and a towel, "Would you like to gargle to freshen your mouth before breakfast, sir?" Seemingly very concerned, Bohdan stared at Jacob.

Jacob thought, "I should not show him, that anything is wrong at all, not to this sly... I must be smarter." After a brief pause he answered, "That would be splendid Bohdan. I drank too much last night, I'm sure my breath is not fresh."

"Mmmmmmh?" Bohdan made a doubting noise, clearly knowing that Jacob was justifying his lies to himself.

Jacob gargled and almost threw up. "Is this some kind of alcohol, or poison?"

"A home remedy to disinfect and freshen up," Bohdan responded.

"I guess you'd know better," mumbled Jacob. "Coffee please, hot." As he said 'hot' he thought of the cold body of old Knyazhna.

Bohdan paused a brief moment, then sarcastically suggested, "How about pants and shirt to start with?"

"Ha, Ha," reacted Jacob, then reminded himself that Bohdan was only a servant, so he lifted his chin and proudly took his pants and shirt that Bohdan held out for him. "Right. Coffee," repeated Jacob.

"As you wish, master," submitted Bohdan.

Jacob sat and ate, trying to match his thoughts to his chewing. "Why did he call me master? Is it because I might become a real master of this castle or is he mocking me? Or God forbid, he knows that I slept with old Knyazhna and now I am the Master?" Jacob continued to eat and think.

Bohdan picked up Jacob's suitcase, "Going somewhere? Master Jacob."

"Just wanted to take it outside for some fresh air. My room has a pretty stale smell and I couldn't even open the windows," Jacob explained hastily, which was close to the truth about the room's condition. Then said to himself, "That was well done."

"Well done, sir," said Bohdan.

"Why would you say 'well done', Bohdan?" Jacob asked surprised and now suspected his mind to be read. He carefully thought to himself, "It is possible Bohdan overheard me speaking of what I thought I was thinking?"

"Well done, was for you dressing so fast."

Jacob ate a little bit more and wrapped some food in a napkin. Putting it aside he caught Bohdan's stare and explained, "For the rats." As soon as Bohdan took the empty dishes into kitchen corridor, Jacob grabbed the food, his suitcase and rushed outside.

EUROPEAN CASTLE, COURTYARD - DAY

The very moment Jacob stepped outside and inhaled, the door slammed shut behind him. It did not startle him because he expected something like that to happen. The clear sky made Jacob feel optimistic about his escape. He began pretentiously shaking his clothes. Ensuring that there was no one there to stop him, he rushed to the gate and found the exact same stick he thought he had lost in the fog. Jacob grabbed the stick, gently opened the gate and poked the soil. It felt as solid as stone.

"So what the hell was that the last time in the fog? This ground is now as solid as stone," Jacob said out loud to himself. He stepped over the iron frame, continued outside the gate and away from the castle.

EUROPEAN CASTLE, OUTER GROUNDS – DAY

Before moving further forward, Jacob continued to poke the ground in front of him and counted his steps in full voice, "Six, seven, eight, nine..." He paused not knowing why he was counting. He turned around and noticed no one was chasing him, "What am I trying to see back there? Why would someone chase me? I came of my own will and I am breaking the contract with my own will. It was just some weird misunderstanding. We simply did not fit." He began to count optimistically, "Ten, eleven, twelve, thirteen..."

Jacob suddenly stopped. Hearing a powerful whoosh behind him, he quickly looked back finding only a wall of fog. "Huh?" Jacob scrunched up his face, questioning the nature of the sound. He poked the stick onto the path that he had just left behind. It felt solid. He decided to prove his contradicting observation to himself, so he rotated 180 degrees and made a step to go back. Abruptly, the soil under his foot shifted, broke and sent him sliding down a steep cliff.

CHAPTER 13

FREEDOM BEHIND THE FOG

FIELD - EVENING

Landing at the bottom of the cliff, Jacob tilted his head up and saw absolutely nothing except the wall of condensed fog. The wind rushed the clouds together to assist in a gloomy sunset. "Hope there's nothing hostile on my way to civilization. I truly hope, or pray, or whatever others say in such situation," Jacob articulated to no one. Encouraged, he stood up and proceeded toward freedom.

Finally leaving the chasm, Jacob traveled onto flatter ground. Yet, when the sun was on its way to retire for the day, he began to hear huffing sounds of unknown origin. Then, there was an abnormally loud, rapid, convulsive blow, like a violent exertion. A mere ten meters behind was a giant bull ready to charge anyone in its way. Out of instinct, as he had no experience of dealing with such situations, Jacob dropped his suitcase and ran for his life, he didn't look back.

FIELD, GATE - EVENING

Chased by the beast's heavy steps and loud breathing, Jacob ran on his last drop of strength. Suddenly, he almost collided into an old style village gate made of a few branches tied up together. Not really hoping much on its help to stop the giant bull, he scrambled through the gate, then stumbled forward ten paces. Not hearing the fence break, he finally looked behind. The sun was done and the roaring beast backed up until it completely disappeared into the night.

"Jesus," Jacob whispered, "Go away you son of a... you nasty beast!" After yelling in pseudo victory, he moved deeper into the gated area, waited, then proceeded forward purposefully. Nature grew silent. "Hello? Anyone? Hello?" Jacob weakly and quietly called out in fear of awaking another animal.

Soon the last bit of enthusiasm left Jacob. When the strength wavered from his legs, he fell onto his bottom and cried like a lost little boy. Seemingly mere moments later, he felt ill in his muscles and more so in his spirit. His forehead dripped with sweat, the cold penetrated his back and his chest was on fire. "That's normal," he touched his head, "I was running from that monstrous bull. Of course I am sweating." Jacob took three slow deep breaths to calm himself and mumbled, "Of course its only normal after what I went through." While he tried to make sense of what was happening, a penetrating chill pierced his entire body, "I must be getting a fever. I must find a place to stay, I..."

Trying to roll over he touched the encircling grass which now held ice pellets. Through dismay, he looked around and saw a heavy frost that permeated the surrounding land. The totality of the events made his eyelids heavy and they began to close.

"I must make myself get up!" moving his dry lips, he slowly pushed himself up and stood on weak legs. A white blanket of snow spreading far forward was revealed in front of him, "I must make myself walk. The question is, forward or back?"

As he looked behind, he saw the horror of a gigantic wave of a snowstorm that was about to swallow him. Against the heavy resistance of nature, he forcefully stepped with his weary legs, onward. From nowhere a bat flew over him, seemingly intending to claw his head. Jacob swung his hands up but the bloodthirsty bat scratched him anyway. Then a carrion crow hovered above him crying the most disturbing cry.

"Go away, leave me alone, go, just die, go!" before he finished the phrase, the crow fell in front of him dead. Losing his balance, Jacob managed to step over the crow and then as fast as he could with his exhausted body, he ran. Snowflakes slammed against the back of his head pushing him forward. He wanted to see where the storm was behind him but was afraid that he would not be able to turn his weary body back. After a short while of running, the frost became thinner and finally disappeared from underneath his feet.

Unexpectedly, Jacob noticed a flickering light not too far ahead. He was not sure if it was a mirage or an actual flame, but he was sure of one thing; he must not stop. Continuing the battle for his life, Jacob was moving closer to the flickering hope that looked like was coming from a small glass window in a small house. Nearly reaching his mirage, he discovered that the flame was real as well as the house. Dragging his feet onward, Jacob cried through his fever struck eyes.

FIELD, OLD SMALL HATA - NIGHT

Jacob stood not far from a small village house. The low to the ground old Ukrainian house, 'Hata' was made of shell stone and yellow clay. The building was decorated with simple traditional painted designs around its edges and windows. It was almost identical to the image Jacob saw in the travel brochures Liz gave him. A few areas near the house were still covered with snow and frost. Jacob impatiently stepped forward, but his foot suddenly stuck in something slimy. It looked like mud. There was a strong scent in the air, "Smells horrible, like an animal farm. That's really good. If this is a farm, there are people." Yet, in such darkness, it was useless to look farther. Noticing a stone path that appeared a few steps from him, as if someone just shoveled away the snow, Jacob pulled his foot from the mud and stepped forward. The path led right to the front entrance of the house.

Reaching the door, Jacob looked through the small window next to it. There, in a very simple century-backward yet pleasant setting, was the warmth that he longed for. He knocked on the window but no one answered. So, he knocked on the door harder and again no answer. "Hello, May I come in? I am coming in," he pushed the door open, stepped in and fell on the floor.

Some time passed before Jacob returned to his senses. First, he closed the door to prevent the valuable warm air from escaping. Instinctively, he walked to the middle of the room toward the heat producing built-in oven, that extended from the wall. It was a traditional Eastern European stone fireplace called 'Peechka' with an opening for placing branches and cooking in the top metal plate. It looked very similar to the one in the castle's bathing room. Warmed up, Jacob looked over at the table next to the window, where a kerosene lamp lit someone's dinner. He stared at the baked goods and a large pot of a rich fatty smelling broth with large chunks of meat in it. Unable to suppress his hunger, he grabbed a chunk of meat and scoffed it down. Distracting himself, he looked around, there in the darkest corner was a narrow bed. With a brief moment of clarity, Jacob sat at the table and waited for the owner of a house. No one came, so he attacked the food like a savage. He shoveled a vegetable filled 'pirogue', an Ukrainian baked pocket-sandwich the size of his hand, into his mouth and ate as if his life depended upon it. And it probably did.

Stuffing into his mouth the last corner piece of crust of the last pirogue he almost choked. Needing a drink, he questioned the contents of a large bottle of a cloudy white liquid on the table. Finally, he reached for it and drank. The strength of the alcohol, made him gasp for a few moments. Jacob scooped out another large chunk of meat and ate it right off the bone, thinking, "Why not?" Locating a big wooden spoon he tasted some bullion, then swirled it. A large part of something in the pot stopped the motion. He wedged the spoon on the side and levered it up. It was a pigs face complete with nose, ears and eyes. Jacob dropped it in frantic terror, he staggered back in shock, and sat on the bed. His eye lids wavered, he leaned onto his side and instantly fell asleep to the sound of the cracking and popping of the fire inside the stone oven.

OLD SMALL HATA - MORNING

The sound of an oinking pig awoke Jacob in petrified confusion from a sleep that could have been compared to a wounded soldier, who was incomprehensibly near death and recovered many weeks later. He opened his eyes and saw the face of a live pig with blood dripping from its mouth staring right at him. Jacob exhaled, his breath mixed with the freezing air became fog, distorting his vision. Holding his fear, Jacob slowly pulled his feet under him then jumped up on the bed and backed against the wall. The pig squealed and continued eating bloody pieces of raw meat on the floor.

Jacob grabbed one of the ears of corn that was hanging to dry above the bed, and threw it at the pig. It ran out through the open door. More of the chilling cold gushed into the house. The penetrating bites of frost urged Jacob to close the door. At his first step down off the bed, he heard the crackling sound of frozen water. He looked under his feet and saw thin ice over a rusty liquid. With his next movement forward, the frozen layer began to crack and a pool of blood burst through, covering Jacob's feet.

Jacob rushed toward the table where the trail of iced-over blood ended. There, he discovered parts of a freshly killed pig with hot steam still rising out of its flesh. Jacob backed up until there was no where to move. By touch he recognized the stone oven and reflectively yanked his fingers off, but then realized it was long cold, "Ice cold? How is it possible? It was blazing hot a few hours ago," he forced himself to recollect last night's events. "Maybe I was here longer than I thought? Or maybe..?" He checked inside the oven and found no sign of fire from last night or any night before. There was not even dust in it. In the corner, right at the level of his head, he noticed the same stick he used to poke the soil near the castle. His tension heightened when he looked down and saw that the stick was stuck in the middle of a freshly killed pig. Jacob was speechless, and tiredness swept over him again when he found his hands covered in dried dark red blood.

OUTSIDE OLD SMALL HATA - MORNING

Delirious, Jacob walked out of the hata. Feeling obligated to whom ever was watching after him, he resumed his journey. Fresh air pronounced calm silence. He squinted from the sun reflecting off of the snow and noticed a group of natively-dressed villagers in white, that passed right in front of him.

"Good morning, people, hello!?!" he called out in elated relief. The villagers continued to pass by without seeming to notice him, leaving footprints in the snow, before dissolving into a wall of thick morning fog. The fence, that he remembered the night before being so far from house, was now a mere ten feet away. Jacob went forward, and through the dissipating fog on the other side of the fence he saw another group people staring at him. They were crossing themselves and whispering to each other.

The crowd began to shout and point at him, "Satana! Satana! Satana!"

Jacob walked toward the crowd but they moved back. As soon as he crossed the gate, the faces of the God-fearing villagers turned to monstrous beasts ready to tear off his flesh alive. Finger pointing, exaggerated arm movements and boisterous yells began to swell, feeding off each other. The shock of the violent mob-mentality scared Jacob into a run.

Reaching an invisible border of seasons, separating snow from green grass, Jacob's vision suddenly darkened. He fell on his knees and then onto his side, curving his back with his limbs drawn in to his torso, into a fetal position.

CHAPTER 14

THE RETURN, HELL IS SWEETER THAN FREEDOM

EUROPEAN CASTLE, COURTYARD – NIGHT

Slowly opening his eyes to the ear-piercing sound of rusty metal, Jacob found himself on the ground at the familiar gate of the castle. In distorted comprehension, he tried to ascertain if what he saw really was. Jacob continued moving his consciousness in search of any obvious clues and finally his blurry vision stopped at the familiar up-turned slippers. He followed the dark dress up to the well acquainted colorless face of old Knyazhna Zoryana. She looked paler and weaker than before.

Knyazhna showed no apparent emotion toward Jacob's return, as she narrated,

> *"It is one of those feelings when you give up on painful incidents, hoping that all of it is just a sleep-trip and you wish to wake up in the convenient safety of a peaceful, boring life."*

No matter how Jacob was happy to get away from the wilderness, in his mind, he blamed old Knyazhna for all his troubles, "God knows what this hell witch is up to." He continued more respectfully, "What is dear Knyazhna preparing for me? Maybe a bath? Or perhaps, Jacob stew?" His guesses rambled, then his self-preserving-senses kicked in, and he whispered with his frost bitten lips, "I found you, Majesty Knyazhna Zo-rya-na."

Knyazhna said nothing. Standing there unmoving with crossed hands with one hand supporting the other like a sentinel at the gate, she did not blink nor took in a visible breath.

Jacob pleaded, "May I come in? Or crawl in," he chuckled hopeful, "Please, I am very tired..."

"If you wish, of your own will," said Knyazhna coldly. Barely separating one hand from another, she gestured inside into the lifeless courtyard.

"There are circumstances," Jacob's words barely

came out as he swallowed, "But my own sincere happiness to see you is now conscious." Tolerating the pain from the inflamed cracks on his lips, he forcefully stretched his smile.

"Welcome," Knyazhna answered in a strong whisper.

Jacob pushed his arms against the ground, separating his body from the soil, and slowly raised himself to an upright position. Astounded by his unexpected potency, he began walking with his own two feet. After a few steps, he felt like skipping in the air, as if he was being pulled up by his shoulders.

"God," whispered Jacob.

"Don't say that word," Bohdan's voice whispered in his ear.

"Huh?" Jacob turned and like many times before, the usual goose bumps ran all over him, he saw no one behind him, not Knyazhna nor Bohdan.

"Don't turn or you might not be able to turn back," Bohdan's voice continued from nowhere. At this point, Jacob knew that everything within these walls challenged his comprehension, yet outside the gate was beyond tolerable, even for his used to be rebellious nature. Jacob tensed his facial muscles and turned his head toward the castle's entrance.

EUROPEAN CASTLE, LIVING ROOM – NIGHT

The dining table was arranged in its usual prosperous way. Yet, this time the atmosphere in the living room, including the dining area, held the gloominess and coldness of a mausoleum. It seemed that the rules might have changed as the routine pre-meal washing was no longer forced on Jacob. He remained as he came, dirty, covered in blood, and with the odor of sweat, grime and God knows what.

They sat silently for a long whole minute at opposite sides of the table. Knyazhna began breathing ponderously, "This blood on your hands..."

Jacob stared at her wondering whether she was a real witch and would she eat him alive, if he blinked. But he protected the looseness of his tongue with the tight pressure of his teeth. He looked at his hands and then wiped the running liquid off his lip. It was blood.

Knyazhna kindly reassured him, "And the blood around your mouth is only the blood of an animal."

While watching Knyazhna from across the table, Jacob analyzed her horrible look, which was much worst than when he had first met her. Her skin was not only pale but had hues of blue, green and gray. Her posture was stooped twice as low, while her hump seemed twice as tall. She now had only two top teeth left and no hair.

"I was under a great distress worrying about your wellbeing, Jacob. Losing you from my sight affected elements inside me," Knyazhna breathlessly delivered.

"I don't understand what that means, change of elements. But I am so sorry for causing you such distress with my behavior," Jacob apologized sincerely.

Knyazhna rose from her chair and walked along the table toward her missed guest. Jacob moved to assist her but she declined with a gesture of her weak hand. He almost knocked over the washing bowl, that was not there a moment ago, and now was situated next to him on a stool. Awakened with optimism that he was still welcomed, Jacob guessed to himself, "All could be the same inside these walls? All can be good?"

Knyazhna reached his side and added hot water for him to wash. With obvious signs that taking care of Jacob gave her great pleasure, the anemic Knyazhna lifted the washing bowl and placed it in front of him. She wetted a white cloth and gently wiped his face, "Let me help you, to wash this blood off of you. It does not suit your innocent look." Her mummified hands touched his bloody cracked lips with her sharp finger nails. As Knyazhna was washing off the blood from his face, the water turned more and more red. Against all the oddness of the situation, Jacob enjoyed it, whether it was from exhaustion or from a trance, he didn't care.

Finally, Jacob stated, "I don't see Bohdan." He did

not hear an answer from Knyazhna and assumed she did not hear him, so he insisted, "Your servant, Bohdan. Where is he? He spoke to me today?"

"Did he?" she questioned and offered, "You must eat something. You need to gain your vibrancy to assist me in my creation."

From Knyazhna's considerate care, Jacob suddenly felt drowsy. He forced himself to speak, but his sleep-deprived state prevented his tongue from sounding sober. Finally, Knyazhna gestured to the dark corridor and a tall hooded figure came over with rinsing water. The hood was so deep that it looked like there was no head inside at all.

"It's not Bohdan is it?" Jacob asked.

"No," answered Knyazhna dryly as the hooded faceless figure carried away the bloody bowl.

Freshened up, Jacob guzzled wine, ate soup, fruit, meat and enjoyed the tingling comfort of his body. "So, what happened to Bohdan?" sudden awareness struck him, "Is he gone?"

"He will come around."

"When?" asserted Jacob with a facade of frightful toughness, though his nerves were not expecting an answer.

"When it is time," said Knyazhna confidently.

"It seems all roads lead back to your castle Majesty Knyazhna Zoryana," he stated through an ever-growing drunken state, "I fell down, I was running forward, yet I dropped back."

Knyazhna's eyes sparkled with the blackness of death,

> *"All roads on soil, sand or sea lead to only an end. To an inescapable demise. People have to choose a path with their own will, in an active way or by passively waiting. All other simple or most elaborate designs of human plans are an illusion."*

She sipped her drink and mourned as if the executioner was on its way.

Jacob moved in his seat and spoke, "Knyazhna, I am having trouble following many things you say, however I am full of gratitude for all of your care. But, I must be truthful. I doubt trusting you because of my constant fear of unknown happenings." He tightened his mouth as if someone was trying to pull it apart.

"To me, fear may not compete with gratitude, therefore, I wish to hear the doubts that chain you against trusting me."

"A few," Jacob said overcoming his anxiousness, "Prior to coming here, I researched your name and there was no such writer," he paused, "nor person."

Knyazhna's reply was calm and rational, "If you suspected falsification in your assignment, why did you come?"

Jacob already had an answer prepared for such an inquiry, "For the reward of course."

Knyazhna studied Jacob for some time before responding. "Then reward you shall receive. As well as the answer," old Knyazhna Zoryana continued with a soft lustful dense breath. "I do not possess a formal education in this specific field and have no desire to compete in academic writing. My simple wish is to deliver a story composed of human thoughts in an ongoing research with the agony of what I learned by being human. All will be perpetuated in a non-edited hand written manuscript." She inhaled, "The meaning of my first name Zoryana is 'constellation', stars that form a mythological figure. My other names are many names, their predominant weightiness is too great for you to learn."

Jacob finish his third glass of wine and stood up, "And last, Majesty, I must know what you were doing in my bed?"

"Subconscious guilt of things that you are ashamed of, they are a brutal rape of the mind supported by imagination which hounds you in bed

at night,"

Knyazhna answered poetically.

Jacob backed a few steps away from the chair and whispered, "What were you doing in my bed? I must know, if I am to stay."

Knyazhna did not appear to be the least bit surprised and replied as if she had prepared the answer a long time ago, "You'll stay. However, one who perceives with doubt, strives for explanations that they want to hear, so you will hear again. I came to comfort you. In your sleep you cried like a wounded beast that is not aware of what it is. Inhuman souls would tremble from that cry. You ran not from my attentive hospitality, but from the remnants and disgust of your conscious good. Most of us learn to bury it away during our indoctrination into adulthood in the framework of mortality." Knyazhna finished, sounding annoyed as if she had explained this a million times before, and gestured for Jacob to leave her sight.

With the lessening of his suspicions against Knyazhna, Jacob submissively walked up the stairway. He entered the bathing room to wash.

EUROPEAN CASTLE, BEDROOM - NIGHT

Clean, the moment Jacob comfortably tucked

himself into his bed, an unwished-for knock startled him. The door opened and old Knyazhna slowly walked in. She sat on the bed next to him with a motherly smile that seemingly resolved all of their disagreements through her forgiveness. In a soft tone, Knyazhna offered to perform her skill, "My inheritance included a sacred ritual, it is the application of common sense to common problem. The demolition of devastation. It may free you from the piercing disturbances of the day, to alleviate the burden of restless nights."

With an apparent semi-cognizant gaze Jacob agreed in poetic form, "I am exhausted by not being able to simply enter sleep but even more so, by falling inside torturous night visions." Finally trusting Knyazhna, Jacob let himself submerge into a dormancy of hypnosis. He had never admitted to anyone what he now admitted to this frightening old woman, that he was not indifferent and not free. Most of his life circling in starry Hollywood, Jacob acted cool and independent. He perfectly knew that the weak are doomed not to survive in the jolly land of dreams.

Knyazhna began the ritual by raising one hand above Jacob's forehead, while pressing a sharp finger nail against his heart with the other. A small drop of blood appeared and covered her nail,

"I force the sigh of anguish, recall the abandonment of your torment and make it heard by you. All you

have hidden from yourself must be brutally exposed."

Jacob could feel his skin become clammy as a frog. His legs were first cold then on fire, then all of his body turned stiff. Knyazhna took a mirror and placed it in front of his face. Jacob glanced in it and saw nothing. Knyazhna knew that Jacob understood the meaning of this nothing; it was the wound where he tucked away the disgust of his own almost wasted life, too deep for others to see yet too near for him to feel.

Knyazhna continued,

"Let the agony of humiliation pulsate your conscious thought, and let the rush of blood through wiry veins flush you toward the final run, your destination of denial."

Out-of-body, Jacob watched himself lying in a puddle of mud from which hundreds of hands had risen from underneath, pulling him down. Sharply falling back into himself, he began to sink into the foul smelling mud. All he could see was shuffling ankles and the feet of a laughing crowd that surrounded him. He implored for help. The crowd continued to laugh.

"Such a recreation of 'primitivism' such simplicity of exposing the inner filth of guilt. I expected something more exquisite," Jacob thought, as he began gasping for air through the slimy dirt that conquered his ears and mouth, turning into stale blood.

CHAPTER 15

LADY LIDIYA

EUROPEAN CASTLE, BEDROOM – EVENING

The vigorousness of Jacob's awakening burst as if he had restfully slept for a year. By touch, he inspected around him trying to find traces of something, perhaps mud. He found nothing referencing his nightmare. He stood up and tried to open the window, but it was blocked by the outside shutters. He spotted a bucket of nice warm water for a morning cleansing, so he splashed his face while continuing to search for signs of last night's horror. All he found was coldness and a residue of sweat from his body. He washed his torso with enjoyment, changed to clean clothing and enthusiastically exited his room.

EUROPEAN CASTLE, LIVING ROOM – EVENING

Running down the stairs Jacob saw an unfamiliar figure of a woman in a red Renaissance-like dress in the living room, pacing back and forth. Her gown was comprised of a tight-fitting bodice, exposing her shoulders and cleavage, and a full skirt that hung down to her ankles. The woman had perfectly done up hair. Through facial powder, her face radiated liveliness and sexuality. She looked to be in her mid 40s, confident and happy.

"These days it's impossible to guess the age of a woman," Jacob mumbled to himself. As his eyes adjusted to the color temperature of the room, he saw the exact hue of her dress. It was a very deep red velvet, embroidered with large white pearls. Accompanied around her neck was a pearl choker on a red silk base. She seemed to be expecting him.

"Hello. I am not sure how we should be introduced?" Jacob attempted to communicate, forgetting all about the previous night.

"It is passion red, the color of my dress," she merrily broke her sentence with a flirtatious tint to her voice and the intent to bewilder Jacob.

"It is nice to finally see a beautiful face. I mean, I guess that passionate color reflects on your face, such liveliness. Compared to some gloomy company," Jacob paused as he realized the brutal mistake of his flattering yet flawed compliment. "It is mostly just I and Her Majesty Knyazhna Zoryana and her butler Bohdan even though he has recently disappeared," Jacob paused again for a second, understanding that he may have said way too much, "I'm Jacob. I am a guest in this house. Castle. Well more than a guest, a..."

"Well I think we will dine, just the two of us tonight. You may call me Lady Lidiya," she said and extended her hand to him.

Contrary to his disacknowledgement toward these kind of manners, Jacob instinctively kissed her hand. He loved her skin. It was smooth, firm and warm. "I am not against that," he said, acting again as himself, cheerful and stimulating; leaving aside any enriching philosophy. He took his seat at the table.

Lady Lidiya took Knyazhna Zoryana's place as if it was her own and said with admiration, "Knyazhna Zoryana was powerfully beautiful once."

"Old Knyazhna Zoryana? I am sure of it; she had to be. We are all beautiful when young," Jacob agreed, while subtly pointing at himself.

Then Lady Lidiya pointed to an opened page in the manuscript laying on the table in front of Jacob. He looked at the page. Lady Lidiya stood up and stepping away from her chair recited from memory with true sensual emotion,

> *"The blossom of youth, itself is beauty. Mine was manipulated and misused. The return of my love fell on my chest with the weight of stone. My tender devotions were preserved in rock monuments, crushing my heart."*

Finishing her recital, the Lady in deep red ended on her knees embracing herself. She rose up and began to eat a piece of duck while standing tall with a towering carefree smile.

Jacob watched with a gaping mouth. "It is beautiful. Lady Lidiya," he sincerely complimented, not as much for her recitation but for the way she ate and swallowed.

She took her seat and silently finished her diner in a demure, polite manner and then finished reciting the poem from the manuscript,

> *"Hurt creates the unforgettable. The way unrecognized priceless art is celebrated centuries behind its time, alike new life, delivered through excruciating pain."*

Jacob could not eat. All he was able to do was

fixate his stare at the Lady in Red in utter reverence and disbelief of her elegance and liveliness.

"Don't look at me; these are words of Knyazhna Zoryana's from the manuscript in front of you," Lady Lidiya pointed.

"Right, sure," said Jacob.

Watching the relaxed Lady in Red, after actively consuming her meal, Jacob finally returned to his free-spirited desires: to live, to love repeatedly, to enjoy. Jacob was not a fan of all these castle dinners and bed time philosophical conclusions, but he would not mind if she was the one to tuck him in. During dinner, he agreed with everything she said and was pleased with everything.

Lady Lidiya finished a large glass of wine gracefully, wiped her hands on a napkin, picked up her cute velvet embroidered gold purse and offered, "Why don't we go for a walk? A simple, no purpose walk, to breathe, to listen to the sound of anything outside." Utterly breaking with her mannerisms, she burst out with provocative laugher.

EUROPEAN CASTLE, COURTYARD
GARDEN - NIGHT

There was no wind nor even breeze outside. Lady Lidiya directed their tour into the bathed in thick moonlight garden. Distinct in its detachment from a common plant nursery, its rarely interspersed greenery of unkept living bushes were overlooked by the gray skins of well-trimmed dead trees. The castle garden appeared surreal.

"I couldn't even imagine, that here, inside these gated walls, is this spine-chilling and at the same time enchanted romantic garden," Jacob delivered his affection to Lady Lidiya while falling into romance. He paused in front of each tree as an enlightened gentleman, imagining himself in the times of the Renaissance, as a knight, a lord, a king. Jacob sheepishly looked at Lady Lidiya for approval.

She was absolutely amused and her words glided off her tongue in a smooth regal way, "I suspect you are contemplating pleasure sir, Jacob."

"Is it that obvious?" not shying from the moment, Jacob was about to kiss the Lady in Red. Their lips almost touched, but then he stepped back to silently admire her profoundly sexual face.

She elegantly pointed with her soft hand to the ground, "Let us rest on the soil."

Noticing the frost, with which he had a bad association, Jacob hesitated, "I'd imagine its pretty cold."

"With your young soul and rushing blood, the soil will be heated in no time," Lady Lidiya instructed in an erotic and very tempting manner, letting a few long strands of her hair tickle the heat-erupting skin of her exposed shoulder.

Withholding his deep sensual desires toward Lady Lidia, Jacob began to struggle. Insanely, he wished to caress her healthy vibrance radiating from the surface of her cheeks, lips and shoulders. Suddenly, snowflakes the size of paradise apples began to fall from the black sky and his Lady in Red began to randomly catch them in her raised hands, "Snow will become white fur to sustain the warmth of our bodies so we can nourish our souls."

"I don't see why not. I think we can easily sustain warmth with a passionate embrace," Jacob played along. Not wanting to look like a boy, though still feeling cold, Jacob landed his rear on the bitterly chilled ground. Lady Lidiya took Jacob's hands with hers, and blew a fiery breath onto his hands that passed through every fiber of his body.

"I applaud you. You confided me with your emotions and desires," Lady Lidiya said as she rubbed his fingers against hers and then placed them against her chest.

A wave of connection in the form of rushing blood to his loin attacked Jacob, "It's nothing. No it is!" He corrected himself, moving closer, hoping not to break this ideal situation, "You are so alive, your skin, lips. Forgive me, my Lady, your breasts."

"Am I? That is a compliment!" she burst out in loud amusement. It did not take away from her sexuality, quite the opposite, Jacob could not stop watching her body slightly move as she laughed.

"Yes, not like the others in this castle. Cold as if they lived underground in a vault," said Jacob.

"Is that right? Like who?" Lady Lydia giggled undoing her hair. She pulled one of her hair pins out and placed it between her lips.

Jacob was about to lose any remaining self-control from excitement. Everything that Lady Lydia did, every movement or word raised Jacob's temptation to force himself on her. He spoke quickly while his chest went up and down with frequent excited breaths, "Knyazhna's hands are that of a deceased person, and the girl I dreamed of, as if..." He could not believe these words left his mouth, as if Satan of Betrayal was twisting his tongue, "But, here with you, I am sitting on the ground, frozen to its core, being sprinkled by the snow. And I am bursting with..."

"Continue," the luscious face of the Lady in Red moved closer.

"I feel no coldness from underneath," he paused for a moment, "All I feel is a rush of boiling desire of love."

Lady Lidiya took Jacob's hand and moved it toward herself, "It is because there is no coldness. Underneath." She led his hand down, across her torso toward her waist. Jacob yearned for an embrace. She continued to guide his hand passed her body and finally rested it on the ground of their sitting island. By touch, Jacob recognized thick bristles of animal hair. He looked down and saw beneath them a white fur rug.

"Girl in your dream?" Lady Lidiya reminded him.

"Yes, she is so beautiful and young and full of energy, just like me. Yet, when I desired her, the touch and penetration was almost painful, from the coldness of her body," As the words left Jacob's mouth, he regretted his truthfulness.

Lady Lidiya stroked Jacob's leg, then stomach looking into his eyes as she ignored what he just said, "Oh, my dear, what is familiar to you is always much more pleasant. A real touch. Sensual hot penetration. Mutual pleasure is the highest pleasure of all."

Through his heat cracked lips, caused by the overwhelmed sensation of his sexual craving, Jacob could hardly add anything to the conversation, "My Lady Lydia, would it be wrong to say that I am infatuated with you in a deep sensual way? Yet, I am feeling as if I am betraying Knyazhna and the dream girl. How stupid?"

From nowhere, Lady Lidiya handed him a glass of wine. He drank hesitatingly yet fast. Suddenly he felt overly good. He stroked the fur underneath them, it was soft. He looked down, the brittles were no longer short but now long as if the animal hair had grown.

"Knyazhna is only your employer and the girl is

only a dream. Why should you care?" she said forcing wine into his mouth.

Like a little boy with his first taste of love, Jacob almost teared up, "You did not laugh at me for what I just expressed?"

Lady Lidiya kissed Jacob on his hot lips and exposed more of her shoulder, "Who would laugh at a confession of sincere remorse, caused by a self-accusation of treachery of loyalty?" She lowered her body and exposed more of her chest. Jacob hastened to kiss her awaiting skin.

Lady Lidiya whispered into his ear, "Yet, temptation is the easiest way to break human loyalty." The deception of Lady Lidiya's inducement sounded like a song of love. Gently holding her, Jacob laid her horizontally on her back, roughly positioning himself on top of her.

In the hasty eagerness of lust, they rushed into a passionate embrace. After only a few moments she pulled back as if teasing his weak character and said, "To fall into a trap of infatuation intrigues me. Maturity knows how to taste its infinite deepness. Yet it frightens me, knowing it might become a dangerous addiction as only the experienced can see. It may be irretrievable, alike the end on the border of darkness. You should know how much greater my age is than yours."

"It's only age. It is irrelevant to our feelings, my Lady Lidiya," Jacob said as he lowered the weight of his cupidity upon her.

Temperamental appetite of human-nature overcame all cautiousness, hers and his.

In a moment of passionate kissing, an intruding distant howl seemed to authorize the clouds to cover the moon. The expelled reflecting light cast night over half of Lady Lidiya's face, transforming it into old Knyazhna. Lady Lidiya spoke in Knyazhna's voice, "Is it irrelevant? The skin? The look?"

Though the haunting image lasted a split second in Jacob's vision, it was too much for him, and he pushed himself aside, "Huh?!" He looked at Lady Lidiya and her face was hers again.

"What is it now? Please come back," she insisted.

Cold wetness conquered Jacob. He sounded ill as he pointed to an empty well-lit space, "I thought I saw Knyazhna Zoryana beside that dark bush over there." He knew that Lady Lidiya knew that he was not telling the truth. He watched the white fur rug underneath them turn into snow. He got up and helped his Lady Lidiya from the ground. The snow began to melt.

"Is that all you can see? If you are with me, then stay with me. Once a lady reaches her feminine sophisticated capacity, she knows exactly what she wants. In denial of her desires, her docility might turn into merciless rage," the luscious Lady in blood Red whispered to his face.

Jacob tasted the perspiration dripping from his forehead, "I guess I was wondering if Knyazhna is okay."

"Would you like to cross the gate to look for old Knyazhna?" Lady Lidiya retorted, apparently losing her patience.

"I know nothing of what is expected of me there. I would rather stay here, guarded by the walls," answered Jacob honestly. He pulled himself together, grabbed Lady Lidiya, bent her backward over his arm and kissed her on her lips. While he was reaching under her skirt, something white caught the corner of his eye. Still holding Lady Lidiya, Jacob almost clearly saw his beloved Excerptus in her pale dress, at the stone wall. Silence became stronger and the long hair of Excerptus floated up from a noiseless wind.

Jacob was stunned to see that Excerptus appeared to be pregnant. "Impossible. Have I been here that long?" he asked out loud, while staring at Excerptus, who held her belly and stared straight back at Jacob. "Nonsense! It wasn't even real," he defended himself against his guilt.

"What wasn't real for you, might be, for someone else the only real thing,"

Lady Lidiya said and freed herself from his arms.

Excerptus lay on her back near the stone wall.

Unable to take his eyes off her, Jacob could not move from where he stood. His mind failed to separate reality from illusion. Jacob saw a large top stone from the wall fall down onto Excerptus's chest and belly. He recalled, once, when he watched a little puppy crossing a fast freeway having no chance of saving it, he still stared in hope of a miracle. But miracles do not come as fast as cars. The crashing sound of her chest bones and heavy exhale were heard and repeated in echoes across the land.

Finally able to move, Jacob ran over to Excerptus. In vain, he attempted to lift the stone but was unable to and when he let it go it seamed to sink deeper into her chest. He cried like a wild beast. The veins on his forehead were pumping with insanity. With a final roar, he pulled the stone off of her chest, took Excerptus into his arms and screamed, "What do you want from me?! What do you want?! Knyazhna! Knyazhna Zoryana! You told me it was just my imagination, a nightmare! Tell me this is not real! Tell me!" His shout was coarse as if all of his vocal cords tore their strings.

Lady Lidiya compassionately touched him on the shoulder, "You have to let it go. If it is what you wanted it to be."

Holding the beautiful body of young Excerptus with her crushed chest, Jacob scowled at Lady Lidiya in complete shock. He began to speak, as if he had gone mad, with his lips covered in slimy, thick saliva, "What did you say? It is what I want it to be? I don't want it to be her! I do not want it to be her!" Jacob kissed the broken chest of Excerptus, dipping his face into her blood, and cried with tightened teeth, "I want it to be a dead pig!" He said almost losing his breath, "A dead pig. He gently shook the lifeless body of Excerptus, then harder and then lamented aloud, "Aaaaaaaaaahh!"

"To whom are you devoted, Jacob? To Knyazhna Zoryana, to Lady Lidiya or to the young spirit, Excerptus? One must be chosen. To be pleasing to all at once is deceitful. To be loyal to all at once is cheating, is betrayal, is anything but loyalty. It is a violation of faith, it is treason," Lady Lidiya lowered her voice to a whisper, "If this is what you want it to be. Then let it be."

Through tearing eyes, Jacob gazed at the regal Lady in Red as he listened to her. Then, he hopelessly looked back to what he was holding in his arms. It was a dead pig wrapped in a white bloody cloth. He gently laid it down and studied the poor dead animal for a few moments. It brought back the memory of the old village house and the dead pig's face in the pot. He felt disgusted with himself and became convinced of his own murdering nature. Kneeling over the dead pig, Jacob covered his bloody face with his bloody hands and howled in agony, wanting to give his own life for the animal he had just slaughtered. He wished to go back to the spoiled environment of Los Angeles, the big city and to be safe in knowing nothing about killing of living nature for the purpose of consumption.

Miraculously, the pig opened its eyes and its skin healed instantly. It jumped up and ran away. Jacob fell on the ground with an expression of horror and happiness at the same time, "He's alive! He is alive?! Thank you whoever changed it!" Not questioning reality, Jacob screamed uncontrollably, "Thank you! Thank you, I would not be able to carry murder on my heart!!!"

Lady Lidiya applauded and laughed, "It is a she."

Jacob pressed himself against the wall, "What does all of this mean? Who are you? Who is she, Excerptus?!" Jacob asked holding his head in both hands.

"Who would you want me to be?" Lady Lidiya asked lovingly.

"I don't know. I don't know! I want all of this to start from the beginning," he implored.

"From the beginning can not be, your verse in an ancient song, it is not a fairytale,"

Lady Lidiya said.

"Where is Knyazhna Zoryana?! I need to talk to her, I trust her. Please!" pleaded Jacob hysterically.

"Follow me, if it comforts you to be near the old Knyazhna. Hurry."

CELLAR AT THE GRAVEYARD - NIGHT

Lady Lidiya and Jacob crossed the dark garden toward an auxiliary building that held a look-out tower. Beyond it, the darkness made it impossible to see the far outer wall. They walked in to the building and went down a spiral stairway. Lady Lidiya led Jacob by the hand into a long chamber. She stopped at the cellar door and gestured for Jacob to walk inside, "Go ahead I will be right behind."

Hesitantly, Jacob stepped in. His attention was immediately drawn to a small window facing the castle's lower graveyard that was lit by the moon. Lady Lidiya did not lie; she was right behind him. She pointed to a single candle that gave off less light than the moonlight seeping in from the tiny window. There, on the soil floor, laid the manuscript. Lady Lidiya said in an ethereal tone, "The words of Knyazhna Zoryana may provide a new path."

Jacob took the manuscript into his hands and heard a sharp sound of the door locking. The weak flame of the candle barely survived the whiff of draft. "And where do I go from here? Hello!" Jacob shouted once but gave up, as he knew by now it was some kind of sick testing of his will.

Lady Lidiya's voice dripped through the key hole in the lock,

"Danger is the sensor of re-evaluation of necessity."

He returned to the door and knocked on it furiously, "How many times do I have to go through this? I have seen danger. I know what it is!"

Lady Lidiya's voice traveled right above him, "There are places where escape may only be possible through thought."

Jacob knocked with all of his might. The candle flame almost died from his brash movement. In fear of losing his only bit of light, he stopped knocking, walked to the manuscript and began to read,

"To start a new day, erasing strokes of darkness that crossed the pages of your life, is the aim to escape a hounded past. Yet, if there is a growing tree, there will always be shadow."

As he read, he visualized a tree with large roots spreading above the soil, making indentations into the ground with its heavy shadow.

The small candle light barely illuminated the room.

Knyazhna's frail voice took over Jacob's spoken words,

"My destiny presented me with nothing but the pain of loss. The Count of Darkness kept coffins full of rats to feed upon, to hold himself amongst the living. For mortals, the wooden box is the sign of death. It wounds the true human soul with devastating sorrow, pitilessly dragging the mourner's life into the grave. Regrettably, it did it to mine an abundant amount of times. I had to make a decision, to play with death by erasing the shadow at the root of the tree."

Jacob finished reading, looked through the window to the graveyard and saw old Knyazhna Zoryana in a white dress among figures in black. He screamed for Knyazhna and the candle died. He screamed even louder, "Knyazhna Zoryana! I am here! Can you hear me?!" But no sound came out of his mouth.

EUROPEAN CASTLE, LIVING ROOM – NIGHT

Jacob gained consciousness in the main keep's living room, seated at the dining table.

Lady Lidiya sat in Knyazhna Zoryana's chair, "I will be taking care of you for now."

Surprisingly, Jacob's mind was clear for thought, "It was the same thing she said the first time we met." He sat upright and fearlessly asked, "What did you do to Knyazhna Zoryana?"

"Do you not enjoy my company? I crave you and I crave to change you into endless existence," the Lady in Red said arrogantly.

"I have to think about it," he answered proudly as if she depended on him.

"Human behavior is an extraordinary phenomena; it changes as in a doll's play. Through the challenges of trials, you should be getting closer to learning the rules,"

the Lady in Red playfully smiled.

CHAPTER 16

HEAVEN INSIDE

EUROPEAN CASTLE, LIVING ROOM – NEXT DAY

No pain in head or body, Jacob woke up in the most comfortable position in his bed, in his chamber. All looked exactly as it was when he first arrived at the castle of old Knyazhna Zoryana. Even the washing bowl was ready for him. Jacob splashed his face, quickly dressed and rushed down stairs to the living room. The dining table was perfectly set up, but there was no one around.

Jacob sat in his chair and began to eat. He enjoyed his food and the red drink tremendously as a perfectly psychiatrically healthy young man would do.

Interrupting his fast chewing, soft icy hands covered his eyes. Astounded by the certainty of recognition, Jacob said, "Blindly I would recall the fragile nature of this softest touch. Am I to question my awakening or do I aspire to dive inside the mirage of night again? Excerptus?"

Young Excerptus spoke with perfect articulation,

"A dream is only strings of thought, where as sanity is search of sanction. Willful aspiration to overcome the doubts of your desire is what makes you reach the unreachable."

The hands separated and Jacob looked behind; there was no one there. He turned back and saw in front of him, a cheerful Excerptus who sat in Knyazhna Zoryana's chair.

"Even if it is not reality I will not take my eyes off you until you vanish," promised Jacob.

"Is that what you want?" Excerptus determinedly asked with her sweet smile.

"I've wanted you to stay forever since the first vision I had of you. At the moment of losing you, at the stone wall, I wanted to end my existence. And if I survived, a part of me would have died," he was not sure if she knew what he was talking about, but he spoke with genuine sincerity. She listened as if she knew what he was feeling. Jacob could not dismiss the fact of Excerptus's perfect articulation, yet he was not going to confront her on her previous act of not speaking his language. He was happy they could communicate and eternally grateful to whatever power had kept her alive.

EUROPEAN CASTLE, COURTYARD GARDEN - DAY

It was a heavenly sunny day with natural to nature chirping birds, slight movement of grass and the distant noise of the greenery. Wearing her white lace dress, Excerptus sat on top of the castle's gated wall and admired the grayness of the dead garden. She laughed while watching Jacob make attempts to climb, then pointed left to the stone steps carved into the wall. Just like the first time they met, they communicated only by gestures. Using the stone stairway, Jacob fearlessly walked on top of the narrow and dangerous wall to join Excerptus. Like birds on a fence, the two of them sat on the wall, content, gazing out to the graveyard. For a while they did not speak.

"I'm very sure of my feelings now. I belong here with you, only, secluded from the rest of the world," Jacob's poetic expression flowed gently like a song.

"Each word has an actual weight of consequence," Excerptus confronted him with penetrating pupils the color of sky.

Then Jacob remembered what he said in admiration to Lady Lidiya in this same garden, "You are so alive, your skin, lips, forgive me, my Lady, your breasts, not like the others in this castle, cold." For a brief moment, he felt embarrassed and insisted on assuring his tested feelings toward Excerptus, "I swear on my heart, I mean every letter of my words."

"I wish you did. And what does it mean, to swear on your organ?" she raised her arms up as if to catch a falling star. "What about the loyalty to Lady Lidiya's heart? What about the gratitude for the gained knowledge you possessed from Knyazhna Zoryana?" Excerptus's demeanor changed and became stoic.

"Good God! How many times do I have to hear that? I believe, no, I am sure of it, that my journey here can only be justified by meeting you. Not to learn from psychedelic experiments that were forced on me by that old lunatic Knyazhna and her lustful aging guest, red Lidiya," he answered as an over-powering 1950s male would answer to his housekeeping wife.

"Forced?" she questioned.

"Yes forced! I am an innocent escort; it's a profession where I come from. By contract I inspire people in art or personal matters for equitable, fair profit," Jacob began to explain to Excerptus, who clearly had zero understanding of outside life and terms. "An escort is a well-paid young male or female to show off with and to spend a good time with. By contract, I was hired by old Knyazhna to be a muse for her writing. I did not sign a contract to be a Guinea pig for psychological experiments. I didn't promise my life to her," he angrily said in part to convince himself.

"Every contract has text between the lines that you must read," advised Excerptus.

Jacob recalled that he did not read the contract at all, as he had never done it before. He was a freelance free-spirited enthusiast of verbal agreements.

"If you wish to stay with me. I must own your life. Just I. For endless eternity," Excerptus demanded as would a young wife entering into an idolized perfect marriage.

"As absurd as this old-fashion vow sounds, it seems there is no exit from this land. If for an eternity to be near you, in my right mind, I pledge my wish to be..."

She interrupted his enthusiasm with a long warm kiss, "It will be a tormenting experience. Transformation is a bitter test. I wish you first to see it." Excerptus jumped from the top of the wall and floated like a feather down, gently landing on the grass.

Imitating her, Jacob jumped but fell down like a rock. Tolerating the pain by holding his lips tight not to wail out, he watched the joyous Excerptus run to the castle.

EUROPEAN CASTLE, CORRIDOR - DAY

Jacob rushed through the dark corridor to follow the fast running, giggling Excerptus. They turned in a direction unknown to him and continued for some time. She stopped next to a wooden door and placed her finger against her lips for him to be quiet, and whispered, "Come in, quietly."

Jacob walked into a pitch black room. As many times before, the door shut behind him abruptly, but this time he sensed he was not alone. Soul-paralyzing, moaning sounds accentuated the dreadful smell of rotten blood. Afraid to move, Jacob nervously spoke out, "Hello? Very funny! Ha, ha, ha! Don't be afraid whoever you are." Without the delay of surprise, Jacob felt heavy breathing on the back of his neck. He spun around skipping a heartbeat. There face-to-face with him appeared the long lost butler Bohdan. Bohdan's face was lit only by a trace of daylight coming through a tiny crack in the wall. Jacob saw an inhuman look in Bohdan's eyes but whispered to him in a friendly way, "Hah. I was looking for you Bohdan. What've you up to?"

Without exhaling or inhaling, Bohdan tried to extend his neck. Apparently his arms and torso were restrained. To say it softly, Jacob's body went numb from head to toe, as if he was going through a massive stroke, yet he had to think quickly, "If I do not distract this ugly savage, he will eat me alive, no doubt." Jacob began speaking extremely carefully, as if he had just seen a coiled snake ready to strike, "How's it go-ing... Bohdy?" He kept his eyes straight on Bohdan, ready to jump back as far as he would be able.

Bohdan began a massive exhalation through his enlarged nostrils. His mouth was glued shut by yellow slimy saliva. Jacob sharpened his mind to a maximum clarity and hastily stepped back just as Bohdan powerfully surged forward. Stronger rays of day light exposed horrifically cracked skin and yellow puss veins on Bohdan's naked body. Bohdan roared like a laboratory beast. "Sh-sh-shit!" Jacob cried and jumped back even further.

The voice of Excerptus shushed them both, "Shuuuusshhh."

Slowly backing up to the wall, Jacob felt a tickle, "A web or small spider," he thought. Overwhelming fear froze him in place, when a more coarse tickling happened again. Jacob turned his neck to look behind. A yellow tongue in the shape of cracked tail of a lizard broke the blackness and pointed at him. The abhorrence that was revealed was worst than any horror movie he had ever seen. Instinctively, Jacob flailed at it and screamed up to the ceiling, "Let me out! Ple-ee-eease!!!! What the fffff! Let me get the damn out of here!!!!!"

"Sh, sh, sh, sh. Don't wake up the others."

Jacob recognized Excerptus's voice. She was sitting to the left of him on a small stool giggling. He slowly moved away from the lizard tail-tongued creature in the dark recess, "Is there any safe spot, even an inch? Please sweetheart, I have had enough psychedelic games, lessons or other shi..... I don't want money or anything to do with your eternal whatever, I just want to leave." Jacob extended his hand toward Excerptus. Like a swift blur, she disappeared. Something else grabbed his arm. He screamed, "Excerptus! Where are you!"

In the opposite corner of the room, the now gloomy Excerptus spoke, "Have you decided? Which one of us?" Excerptus lifted a small portable light. Behind her stood Bohdan and five or more barely visible half-beings, seemingly guarding their darkness and the pungent smell of blood. The rotten gathering stared motionlessly at Jacob.

"God damn it! I don't want anyone or anything, nothing!!" Jacob whispered ill and forcefully.

As if she had heard nothing of what he said, Excerptus spoke in a deep demonic multi-person baritone voice,

"We are chosen, embraced into eternal nobility. We choose to be born by our own will into a deathless life through birthless tissue. We are children of Nosferatu.

We are Excerptus."

Shivering, from what felt like a nervous breakdown, Jacob was losing his defensive capability. He assumed he was hallucinating, "Is this a game or the insanity of a crazy cult trying to influence me to the core of my smallest cell?" The poor cupid boy was declining to understand anything anymore.

Bohdan slowly opened and reopened his sticky mouth, releasing a possessed deep rasp,

"Have you made your decision to give away your vital light for eternal nightfall amongst the awakened?"

"God dam-n, you all! What is this? A, a, a cult? Is this s-ome kind of a bl-oody cult? Or, you are all insane, psychos. What is going on?" through nervous convulsions, Jacob shouted broken words.

"A cult, a sect, what ever you find appropriate to call it from your amateur naive point of view. To us, in this land, in this time of existence, it is 'Gathering of Chosen'," Excerptus explained putting her hair into ponytails.

Jacob accidentally bit down on the inside of his cheeks, moaned from pain and researched through his trembling mind, "I must think quick. I must find the right answer. If this is a cult, I can manage it. If it is in fact some demonic fecal nest, I'll have no power over myself even to think. But I am thinking now. So I am still human." He tried to puzzle his own thought quietly in case someone could listen to it. Finally, he came up with an unmasked answer, "I must obey the rules of the house in which I am a guest, and I must not go against what has always been." He finally answered courageously, "I, I need to think about it, if you would allow me. I understand I must and I do respect the rules of the house. Thank you in advance." He swallowed hard.

Clearly aware of Jacob's lie and desire to flee, Excerptus proclaimed,

"The choices are modest in count. You may choose to be present in the exaggerated human good with its infested widespread plague of calamity, of illness and evil and its underlying sense of the undisputed forthcoming death. Escaping the simple path, is the nominated proposal, the supremacy of the Predominant Ancestry, an endless continuity in the other side of light, as a Child of Nosferatu."

When Excerptus put her light on a stool in the darkest corner, it exposed another group of chained and ill-looking exhausted people. Jacob shivered from his sobering judgment, "Who.... are they?"

Excerptus answered with ease, "Vital vitamins. We

drain them for a few days, a week at most. They don't have much to go. They are wishing for the end."

With his last nerve, Jacob attempted to make a joke, "How sweet. Hopefully, I will not become a Vitamin J."

Excerptus chuckled cheerfully, "You are too handsome for that, J.,

> *'But eventually the strength of youth gives up and allows the negativity of life to drain your health, your energy, your will. Death only comes when life gives up on you. Choose 'Excerptus' or an inevitable grave."*

She pointed indicating for Jacob to leave. Cautiously, he proceeded to the door. In a flirtatious manner, Excerptus exited first and he rushed to follow her. Closing the door behind, Jacob caught the look of the chained Bohdan, who winked at him.

CHAPTER 17

THE MASTER OF THE CASTLE

EUROPEAN CASTLE, BATHROOM – EVENING

Dismissed from the co-inhabitants' presence, Jacob was allowed to do as he wished inside the castle walls. Before arriving in Eastern Europe from sunny California, he was not obsessive with his bathing ritual. Of course, the weather did not require layering of clothing and hand sanitizers were offered all around and simply, he did not consider being dirty unless there was dirt on him. Photo session flashes and being showered with gifts and sexual attention only caused minimal stress, which could not compare to these three mental and sexual blood sucking women of different age who made him triple perspire. The previously bothersome house rules of bathing now became a most likable habit for Jacob and even something relieving, like a meditation.

He walked into the bathing room with impatient eagerness and sat on the permanent stool next to a pot with hot water. As customary, he found a platter of grapes, cheese and the red drink. A female hand touched him and began washing his shoulders. Steam made the surrounding area almost invisible. Jacob shivered, knowing not what to expect.

"We must wash out the bad impressions," whispered Excerptus and began to rub Jacob's chest with a rough wash cloth made of roots.

Collecting all of his courage, he asked, "May I ask?"

"Ask," she paused washing and poured the red drink into a silver goblet and placed it against Jacob's lips. He did not expected this, and in an instinctual reaction, pushed her hand away. She dropped the goblet, the spilled drink looked more like blood than wine.

"What is it that you wanted?" asked Excerptus.

"I am sorry, Excerptus," Jacob apologized, stood up and stepped over to pick up the goblet from the floor. "This is what I want to know. There, in the cellar. Those who will not become children of Nosferatu, will you drink their blood?"

"Ha, ha, ha! I thought you grew out of the age of

stories about blood-sucking vampires," Excerptus merrily laughed and touched his shoulder. "Pick up the chalice . It belonged to my creator, centuries ago."

With suppressed reluctance, Jacob reached down and grasped the goblet.

"Some drink blood because they believe it has direct influence on supplying their organs with life bursting nutrients. A shot of blood is known as 'Medical Sanguinaria'. It is claimed that intake of blood has headache, fatigue and epilepsy relieving benefits. Centuries ago the ill drank the blood of the healthy, hoping it would pass its youthful vitality and cure. Blood was considered a medium between the physical and spiritual life. But, yet, all of it, true or not, is effective only for the living body and mind."

Excerptus took Jacob by the hand and walked him to the long bench, where they sat. Jacob recalled the horrid near accident that ended with a sword stuck between his legs. Cautiously, he glimpsed up. Instead of a sword, there above them hung bouquets of dry flowers. Excerptus took a large water cup and poured warm water over Jacob. Strangely, the water ran for a long time, as if it was coming out of a faucet.

"What does that suppose to mean?" he asked again.

Excerptus's answer was clear and direct to the point,

"The power ruling human bones and muscle is not the blood, but the soul. The Subtle Energy is difficult to perceive, mysterious and delicate in intent. And, that is the main source of our power."

Jacob sat there processing her words with difficulty.

LOS ANGELES - EVENING (FLASHBACK)

Listening to Excerptus's narration, Jacob flashed back to a memory of not so long ago. He appeared inside a scene of an upscale party and saw himself as an observer.

The tender mouth of Excerptus continued, "These are the examples of life's daily exhaustion of human energy, where you, Jacob, a character, see yourself as a hero, but in fact you are a victim."

The dynamic Hollywood Hills party was filling up with cheerful, happy, hip and fashionably dressed people ready for a good time. The DJ was changing eras in music, fast and skillfully. It was a warm afternoon turning into evening. Drinks and food were decorated with flowers.

Excerptus's lofting voice walked Jacob through the party, "Remember those friendly smiles and the emptiness in their eyes?"

Loaded with raw boyish energy, Jacob was proudly moving through the crowd, shaking hands with other young and mature men that were passing by unendingly.

Excerptus's voice continued hovering over Jacob like an invisible celestial seraph, "Watch for a friendly hand shake, full of envy, sucking your pride and inner energy. These are human vampires."

Each pleasant handshake with friend or acquaintance weakened Jacob's posture and strength. Separating his hand from his last neighborly mate he felt a sudden thirst. Then, a gentleman appeared with an elegant smirk and offered an honorable hand. Jacob felt his heart slow down. He stopped and placed his drink on a table, "But, most of these people I've known for a lifetime. Family friends, partied, went to college together and shared both happy moments and troubles." For the first time, he noticed something he had never looked for before in their pupils; it was ugly back-stabbing jealousy. He watched the familiar grim people walk away. The realization of their deceitfulness came with the cost of a painful disappointment of friendship.

Dividing the crowd, a sexy long-haired blond with black roots and a predator-like nature was approaching Jacob with a Hollywood air kiss.

Excerptus continued her presentation of the case of unsuspected incidents, "There are the determined ones, those who must make you surrender to them by draining the stability of your muscles through a sensual hug." The black rooted blond attacked Jacob with a hard, prolonged hug. He felt his muscles first tense, then an erection tightened his pants. There, his muscles flopped to the point that he could hardly manage to hold his posture.

"These are people you like, who act as if they like you. And, there are others," Excerptus's voice echoed overhead. A group of people appeared at the horizon of the back entrance. By all attributes, contrary to their high end wardrobe, they were a gang. They advanced toward the already wearied Jacob, who stood there ready to let each of them punch him in the stomach.

Excerptus appeared right behind Jacob, "Here are your obvious enemies that you know of, yet are uncomfortable in turning around and walking away." Step by step in slow motion, the gang moved closer and closer to Jacob. He knew exactly what that meant. He had been in this situation a million times. Inserting into the present-past, Excerptus blew a whisper into his ear that reverberated like in a water well, "Each and every meeting, these cool chilled people fostered their nasty hope, impatient to hear about your ultimate failure. With their hello, they implant bad luck in you, by taking yours. The invading stress detunes your good mental health and sickness of body follows."

"I always knew. I can recall every ill feeling of it, but, ashamed of my unimportance, I could never turn away from them because I would have to admit my 'loser' status," Jacob lamentedly stared right at the gang.

A group of his enemies was ten, eight, six, four and now two steps away. Excerptus stood in front of Jacob, freezing everything around them. Her face turned pale with dark blues circles forming around her eyes and purple veins popping out on her forehead. She screamed in a raspy tone, "Turn around!!! Jacob. Turn and walk away!!! Now!!!" Excerptus dissolved into her paleness, unfreezing the event.

Facing the gang only a step away, Jacob turned and took a first step in the opposite direction.

A tall sexy brunette shouted, "Hey Jacob where are you going? Don't you think you should say 'hi' to people you respect?"

First, Jacob was stopped by some weird energy to which he resisted. Then the sensation of an iron rope around his body pulled him back and he was losing strength. He resisted again and realized that all of it was his own self-created duty of social responsibility. He faced them again, gave them the middle finger and said, "I don't respect you and I don't owe you shit."

Excerptus froze everything again and applauded Jacob,

"These are the darkest of humanity. They live off your pain, failure, suffering and depression. They extract your spirited breath, turning it from the ethereal into a gravestone."

Jacob watched the gang become colorless. Their skin took on a paleness and their eyes gave away to white. Their arms hung stiff and their mouths became black dump holes.

EUROPEAN CASTLE, BATHING ROOM – EVENING

Thoroughly washing and massaging Jacob's body, Excerptus poured rinsing water over him and then positioned herself on his lap. She began to elucidate facts that were impossible to examine or contradict,

"Children of Nosferatu shall not murder the pure, but receive the light of their spirit through draining those who usurped innocent victims. We are an aid of humanity."

She placed Jacob's hands over her hips.

Jacob knew exactly what she expected from him,

but was uncomfortable to acknowledge the powerlessness of his manhood, "I don't think I can be sensual after being experimented on so much."

"Of course you can. Pain and sorrow are the strongest aphrodisiac for the lust of love," she blew out the lamp and darkness engulfed them.

"Remember how you, me and all of those monsters were in the same cellar?" Excerptus whispered into his ear. Jacob made a young healthy aroused noises as she continued whispering, "And if you give me what I want, I'll give you what you want, eternal power over mortality."

In the darkness, sounds of ecstasy were beginning and ending, ending and beginning.

EUROPEAN CASTLE, BATHING ROOM – DAY

Jacob woke up on the floor of the bathing room where he was washed and pleasured the night before. Through the tiny window he recognized daylight but was not sure of the time. The outer pain of his skin and muscles, especially on the side where he had apparently fallen asleep, was strong and permanent. Yet, he felt a foreign emptiness inside his body, as if he did not have any inner organs.

Tentatively, he stood up from the wooden floor.

The bathing room was still warm and there was hot water in the pot prepared for him. Jacob washed with great enjoyment, periodically plunging his head into the pot. Calmly he rinsed off the scented soap he had grown fond of. He found a towel and his clothes ready for him.

"Hopefully, this was all a nightmare, well maybe not all of it. I'll keep the ending," he was aroused again.

EUROPEAN CASTLE, LIVING ROOM - DAY

Meticulously dressed and bursting with incredible joy, Jacob rushed down the stairway to the dining hall. Corresponding to his mood, his perception of the room's aura was calm and welcoming, and he wanted to defend it tenderly even if judged by a large opposing gathering. There to Jacob's favorable wonder, the table was set up identically to the first time he had walked into the castle. Old Knyazhna Zoryana awaited him in her chair. Butler Bohdan, relaxed in his own way, stood nearby.

Not wanting to restrict his bliss, Jacob exclaimed cheerfully, "Dear Knyazhna, your Majesty Zoryana! I was sick with worry about you! Where have you been?" He rushed right to her almost tripping. Bohdan stopped Jacob's enthusiasm and made him bow. Jacob did not resist. This day he was feeling new, he dismissed all the horrifying experiences as nightmares. He was one hundred percent aware of what he learned and concluded about the rules of this house.

"Please Sir Jacob follow etiquette. Bow and take your seat," ended Bohdan with a rasp steady tone while fidgeting on his feet.

Jacob winked at Bohdan and said, "Bohdan! I had the weirdest dream about you as well," and added, "I hope it was only a dream."

Bohdan threw a penetrating look at him, "As you wish, Sir."

"May I give Her Majesty Knyazhna a hug first?" requested Jacob and moved forward. Bohdan stopped him with his ice-cold gloved hand. Bohdan's face showed nothing and to decipher it was a waste of time.

Jacob stepped back, bowed low to the ground and thought, "And what old Knyazhna is planning for today even the All-Mighty of Light or Darkness could not say." Having no plans or negative thoughts for the first time in many days since his arrival, he simply looked forward to a late brunch. He remembered what Knyazhna and Lady Lidiya taught him, "See what you wish to see." All he wished for was a meal and the stress relieving home remedy of humans, alcohol.

"Majesty Knyazhna Zoryana," Jacob tried to see if anything was different, about Knyazhna Zoryana but found nothing different only incredible power in her posture. He bowed again and walked to his chair. Knyazhna said nothing until he reached his seat.

"It is a pleasure to see you again, Sir Jacob," she welcomed him with a voice full of strength.

"Alright. Goody, goody," mumbled Jacob, who was already visually picking at the food and ready to dismiss everyone. He made himself comfortable in his chair and began to eat.

Bohdan approached Jacob with a hot pot of coffee, "Coffee, sir?"

"Oh, boy! Thanks, sweet Bohdan. You know me well."

"We all know you well, dear Jacob," intruded Knyazhna eagerly, "What an experience you obtained. One you can not purchase for gold. Bravo, young man!"

Jacob let her talk run through his ears. He was sipping his coffee and staring at Bohdan's wrists which had imprints and bruising like from metal cuffs.

After agreeably satisfying his hunger, Jacob confessed calmly, "Every day or night I wake up, I am not sure what is real and it terrifies me, yet..."

Knyazhna interrupted,

"What we see with closed or open eyes, interpreted by our imagination, is our own self-reality. You should have learned that by now, Jacob."

Joyfully chewing, Jacob impatiently disrupted "From now on, I will stop any such guessing and thinking. I have no desire to see myself going mad. I will enjoy what ever it is." He saw Knyazhna's smirk of denial. Jacob felt the slight rise of his anger and decided to say something to avoid an explosion. Because for now, he knew that the game of trying his qualities was not over. He sincerely hoped that his obedient behavior within the constraints of the house rules would give him a chance of ending the berating, at least for a short break, "May I ask a question Knyazhna?"

"All young are full of sweet curiosity, until it becomes a burden," she retorted.

"So may I, or may I not?" Jacob said with slight irritation.

Bohdan interfered, "How much do you want to know, Sir Jacob? What you learn may torment you for an endless time." Bohdan fidgeted heavily on his feet as if his legs were invisibly chained.

"Are you a dark side of existence?" Jacob casually gathered his guts to ask them both, "A contradiction of God, an antichrist? Or, what do you call this reclusive association inside these walls?" he pointed to the inside walls of the castle.

Knyazhna's eyes seemed to recall a thousand years, and she answered as if she was expecting this particular question,

> *"Sadly, God and I have never crossed paths in a moment of agreement. Long before the passage of many seasons, I was young and confident. When I came across intolerable pain, God would not hear me, because in my immature pride I denied his earlier offers. Like a ticking bomb counting down to its explosion, the decision was beyond the given time to choose between death, with its only supposed after-life or to go into forever, under the definite shade of infinity."*

Familiar shivers ran across Jacob's shoulders, so he swigged down his glass of wine. Then he reclined in his chair, held a moment of silence and spoke, "Assuming the case that I'm in your reality and will have to go through all these changes... Bohdan seemed pretty mellow. Why did he have to be restricted with steel chains?" He pointed at Bohdan's wrists, gaining in return a life-threatening look.

Knyazhna raised her chin in an educator's manner, "Very few are able to withstand the changes that open with the knowledge of themselves."

Bohdan looked at Knyazhna and she nodded for him to speak, "You will have to overcome a lot inside these walls, Sir Jacob..."

Knyazhna spoke victoriously, holding her goblet high,

"Unchained, that is a heavy test, my boy."

"It never ends does it?" he stated. Jacob was eating like a savage to cover up his nerves, then asked arrogantly, "What does it mean unchained, chained? Stop threatening me! I have not agreed to become whatever you are." He stood sharply out of his chair, pushed a few items from the table with rage and yelled, "I've had enough with whatever you have been poisoning me with. With the lessons, tests, trials, bloody love and hate, fear or food!" Jacob smashed his plate against the wall, "I am out of here!" He quickly walked toward the exit. Bursting with sick ill-will, Bohdan appeared in front of him, ready to charge like a bull. Bohdan's mummified veins were about to break the surface of his seemingly days old dead skin. Knyazhna lifted her hand to prevent any action.

"What are you?! Some kind of freaks? Mad vampires?! Draculas!" losing his voice Jacob shouted.

With blood-drowned eyes, Bohdan suddenly was holding a well polished silver coffee pot. Seeing his reflection, quietly hysterical Jacob backed up to the wall and stopped because there was no where else to go. He did not know how to escape, so he shut off his mind from imagining horrific things that could happen to him.

Old Knyazhna Zoryana spoke calmly,

"Dracula is yesterday. The past. His power is an open book to the world. His plans, however, are yet a mystery. There is only supposed comprehension of one's forthcoming fate. Inability to validate accurate knowledge of the future, to all, that is real fear."

A familiar feeling of nausea was conquering Jacob and his eyes became watery. He recognized his upcoming weakness and inability to escape, yet he was confident in his right of freedom and protested, "I am leaving now! You have no right to keep me here against my will! I have rights!"

"It is late, Sir Jacob," said Bohdan, who surprisingly now looked and held himself neutral, "Look at yourself. If you wish to leave as it is, do it. You hardly have skills to survive outside." He held the silver pot in front of Jacob again.

Jacob glanced at his face and saw no difference. He touched his face and it felt smooth. He continued his hand down until it was interrupted by the touch of sharp nails. It was old Majesty Knyazhna. She pointed with her lifeless hand at two puncture marks at his jugular and said, "This is your castle, Sir Jacob." Jacob stared at his reflection in the silver and by touch, confirmed the discovery of puncture marks on his neck. He slowly circled backward then landed in his chair unable to speak.

Old Knyazhna sat across the table in a new throne, that was made gem encrusted gold. Her Majesty Knyazhna laughed, as if she was some kind of repugnant, unclean spirit, "Look on the bright side Cupid, you may live forever, in the darkness though. Ha, ha, ha!"

Bohdan smiled joyfully and as lively as he could.

Jacob's survival instinct turned on, as never before, he became alert and said, "I have grown to love you, Knyazhna Zoryana, with all my heart. Just the way you are. Please believe me." But it was not enough to charm the old trickster.

Knyazhna replied coldly, "My revitalized appearance, I owe to myself only. I presented it to you, to open your eyes and see my glory. If I did not have my strong will to overcome the truth of my declined look, you would have never seen anything in me but deteriorating decay. Yet, you inspired me toward a crusade of my rejuvenation. For that I am grateful."

Jacob could not understand the complexity of Knyazhna's words about her revitalization. He saw her change a bit but nothing that was worth such an announcement. He did notice changes in her, outside the range of normalcy and would not be surprised if he saw her glue bits of hair onto her skull or use removable dentures to give the appearance of growing teeth. He concluded that, it was just an old woman's psychosis. Yet for the big picture of survival, he continued to push his charm, "It is difficult to understand someone's feelings, like yours to me or mine to you. However with utmost sincerity I can assure you that every time you were not around I missed you tremendously. I mean it!"

Jacob looked to the far window. The sky suddenly became moody as before, and the coming storm changed the color of late afternoon into night. The moon, confused by the darkness, emerged surrounding herself with defused purple.

Knyazhna continued to express her collective sensitivity as a defenseless elderly woman, "Love, that is most essential to me, you are not capable of Jacob and will never deliver it, not to an old lady."

Jacob perceived Knyazhna's vulnerability and pushed harder to empathize with her sentiment, both with sincere and self-defending intent, "Try me! I beg you Your Majesty. I see things differently now."

"True, you Jacob grew by gaining tiny bits of wisdom," Knyazhna responded with deep tired pride.

The candle near Jacob died as the flame of the candle near old Knyazhna became stronger. It exposed every emotion of unstoppable brutal aging on her ancient face, that long ago was Princes Zoryana, "Twenty years may leave no imprints or traces on the human outer layer, yet one moment may scar for life, maturing an appearance by decades."

A sparkle of tears in Knyazhna's eyes made her susceptibility three times more obvious. Then the dryness of her skin crossed the limit of old to mummified, yet she continued with more potency in her voice,

"Over satisfied in eternal power, the Nosferatu began to taste life as many of the wealthy, desiring nothing exceptional but consuming excessive existence without gratification. Soon, from the boredom of the Nosferatu, emerged a necessity for the yearning of the mortals, the self-torturing pursuit of passion to addiction. Passion in the form of love that almost destroyed all of my predecessors. I believe in no loyalty but dedication to ambition. I find no love but the scientific attraction of chemistry. Therefore, I will not be destroyed by self-created poetic delusion!"

Knyazhna moved a few things on the dinner table

near her, while her gaze nailed Jacob to his seat.

Jacob answered with deluded confidence, "Doesn't matter does it?" He paused, "I guess I will become one of you. Nothing else I can be afraid of."

Knyazhna replied with a intensely dispassionate cold tone, "Not with my help boy."

Jacob swallowed his drink, "Why not? What did I do wrong?"

"You forgot me too soon," she said and bit on a piece of pheasant.

For the first time, Jacob saw old Knyazhna chew well. His mind rushed through options, then he decided to use another of his psychological tools, rejection. In his boyish past, he would resist a woman to make her want him more. Jacob directed his arrogance across the table, "Fine. I will ask the passionate Lady Lidiya. She will appreciate a hot reunion." Then he added extra insolence, "...or maybe I can teach love to the curious, enthusiastic Excerptus. Someone will care enough for me to give me that super endless life."

Suddenly, Jacob's vision began to twirl, and he saw an emergence of pale red throughout the gloomy shade of Knyazhna's attire. Knyazhna's mummified skull began to fill in with muscle and collagen, stretching and forming her skin. Bloody red velvet emanated from her bleak dress. Knyazhna's lifeless face converted into the healthy, full of life, Lady

Lidiya.

Jacob began to cough in reaction to her transformation and the veins on his neck bloated. Bohdan continued to watch him. Finally, Jacob gasped for breath, then hoarsely exhaled and stared at the other end of the dining table, where in the throne of Knyazhna, sat the erotic Lady in Red, Lady Lidiya.

The Lady in Red smiled lustrously, "Not with my help. Why should I, handsome?"

"Lady, My Lady Lidiya. You felt what I felt, what we feel for each other," hurried Jacob.

Lady Lidiya's tone shifted to one of indifference, "I was not interested in your sensual fidelity, Jacob. However, I insisted that your loyalty must be served to one. You rejected my offer so I withdraw my passion."

And then, right there, her stimulating body began to lose its heat, the rose tone of her skin changed to pale.

Her red dress faded to pastel. Jacob watched as the process of declining colors continued and his memory took him back to a romantic date with Lady Lidiya, until the moment of landing on a frozen soil. When he snapped back to the present, he saw a flash of pure white. He could still recognize the pearls from the red dress but soon they became snowflakes. Fixating his vision on the bleaching of the material, Jacob missed the revelation that emerged like a mirage.

Now, instead of Lady Lidiya, the young Excerptus appeared, delicately arranging her lacy dress in the throne of Knyazhna Zoryana. Jacob jumped up, tripping over his own feet, and he scurried away from the table. The fragile Excerptus rose from her seat exposing her well-suited pregnancy under the snowy fabric of her outfit, "Not with my help. You have done nothing that was not convenient for you. That is why you could not choose one." Excerptus tenderly touched her belly and continued,

"The requirement of becoming Chosen is to be able yourself to make a choice, avoiding temptation."

Jacob rushed toward Excerptus and fell on his knees in front of her. From an extended distance, he placed his outstretched trembling hands onto her belly, "You are and you were the only one for me. Always and forever." He whispered affectionately while caressing her belly, "And our child. Our child. It's unreal, a true miracle!" He burst with sincere joy, forgetting everything that had happened up to this moment. Crawling closer, Jacob kissed her belly and pressed his face against it. Embracing his future, he suddenly felt a strange tactile change. He sighed and elevated his head in puzzlement to discover, instead of Excerptus, a pregnant Lady Lidiya.

Jacob hopped up off of his knees and took a few steps back, "And you, too, are pregnant, my Lady Lidiya?"

"A miracle is an extraordinary entity my dearest Jacob," she extended her hand toward him and gently commanded, "Come closer to acknowledge fatherhood."

He swallowed and moved farther away.

"Aren't you happy? For my child? Our child?" Lady Lidiya asked.

"I don't understand. I don't feel well," Jacob clutched his head with two hands.

Lady Lidiya seized Jacob's wrist, pulled him toward herself, and pressed his hand against her belly. He felt a knocking movement under his palm. Jacob placed his ear against her abdomen and heard the heartbeat of an infant. His face changed to gentleness, "What a beautiful sound! My God."

He moved his lips around Lady Lidiya's belly and then listened to it again. There was no more sound. "I can't hear it anymore. It stopped. Where did it go?" he began to cry lamentably as if he had truly lost his own child. Continuing to hope for a sign of life, he probed his head and hands around her midsection. "Why did it stop? Why did the baby's heartbeat stop?" he whispered in heartbroken confusion, "Was it or it wasn't...?"

"Why do you think, Jacob, the beat of the heart stopped?" she asked him in return.

With utter despair strewn across his face, Jacob

firmly placed his palm at her stomach once again, "Because it stopped its existence?"

Lady Lidiya whispered tenderly,

"Possibly because someone was damaged to death from a broken heart, that of loss."

This time, as Lady Lidiya spoke, Jacob watched her through his pain and he saw her beautiful round belly flatten, as her back initiated the inflammation of the hideous protuberance. He then witnessed the most unappealing physical transformation of Lady Lidiya into old Knyazhna Zoryana with her inverted stomach and elevated hump.

The priceless green-hued fur wrapped itself around Knyazhna's neck. Green was her favorite, the color of life. It had never been said that green was an overly complimenting vibrance to lifeless pale gray, as was the skin tone of the archaic Knyazhna. On the contrary, this unfitting palette suited her noble authority.

Emotionally suppressing himself, Jacob held in an attack of hysteria silently. Barely able to speak, he asked, "What are you?" He embraced himself as if he was tied up in a straitjacket, "Am I going to go mad and rot in here? Is that what you want from me? Is that what am I here for?" Looking at Knyazhna's now both blurry eyes, Jacob could not remember which one could see, he cried, "At least you are not pregnant Great Majesty!" He stood up and danced a strange old European dance that he never knew. Sweaty and exhausted, he leaned against the wall, slid down and sat on the floor whispering through dryness that bound his lips, "Why me? What did I do so horribly wrong in life that I have to go through these trials?"

"Self-seeing ourselves is subjective and self-defending. What you said or have done, in a chain of events, could have damaged someone severely. Yet for you, it was simply an emotional expression and you never thought of its consequence ever again. For all we know, you could be an inert murderer. When a conscious struggle emerges from our deeds with the question 'Why am I?' this is an outcome of an enormous progress that brings mankind closer to becoming a more fulfilled 'sapient homo sapiens'."

With his tired, scrunched up face, Jacob resignedly watched and listened to Knyazhna. "What next?" he thought, then said politely. "You still did not answer! Why I!?"

"Why not I?" replied Knyazhna with thick saliva-like tears running from her single blurred eye. Her other eye was now healthy and blue. "Why did I not deserve your fondness? My need of kind friendly attention is no different from the young. What was it that most repulsed you from me?" her oral cavity was turning into a dark tunnel and the blue of her eye was changing to black, "Why had I not seen your sentiment of tenderness toward me?"

Jacob laughed and cried simultaneously, "Are you mad? You are mad! Do you see yourself? Look at yourself!" He grabbed a silver tray and threw it at her feet.

Burdened with her royal blood, Knyazhna seemed to battle her pride after the uncounted insults on her dignity, yet she glanced down at her image in the silver. Her facial expressions were in obvious pain. From nowhere, the familiar owl flew in at high velocity beating the wind, and determinedly stabbed its claws into Jacob's shoulder.

He froze, then screamed, "AHHHHH! Stop! Stop!" With two hands Jacob squeezed and pulled the owl off of his body. He heard the ripping of his skin as the bird took off, flew and sat on the table near him. Fearfully, feeling the wetness of his shirt from the gushing blood, Jacob refused to look at his torn skin. Supporting himself by the table, dizzy, he could hardly hold his head up on his shoulders. Looking down at his feet, he saw a stone. With superior force, rage overpowered the sensitivity of Jacob's unstable mind. He took a slow breath, gradually squatted, grabbed the stone, raised it and began to beat the bird, until the feathers and flesh became one big mess. During his murderous rage Jacob clearly saw flashes of the dying owl's eyes but they did not stop him. The madness had taken over at first but then the damage was too severe that to leave the bird barely alive was a worse cruelty than to kill it.

"Overwhelmed by remorse, Jacob dropped the stone and spread his hands far apart as if being crucified. He continued to search, with his ill mind, for the dead bird's heart. Like a tiny lake, the silver tray laid on the floor between old Knyazhna and Jacob capturing their faces in their explicit states."

A lucid sparkle of a tear, gemstone like, embellished the wrinkled, mummified face of Knyazhna. She whispered, "I have found a very sad reflection of myself in that purity of silver but have you seen yours, Jacob? All I was in need of was the sincerity of a free-spirited, affectionate soul, not the affection of a sincere one. You are too far from being sincere my boy." Showing the suffering of inhuman pain, Knyazhna's mouth turned down in the shape of an accordion bridge in her soggy, dying skin,

"What have you done Jacob? Destroying the innocence of others as well as your own. What have you done?"

Urgently trying to distract himself from the

horrifying crime he had committed against nature, Jacob watched the repulsive mouth of the old witch. He was ready to be sucked into that black hole forever, to forget all that had happened to him. He followed where her long fingernails directed him to the table of the execution. He hoped he was hallucinating when he saw the owl's eye still looking at him. Then he focused his distorted vision to meticulously dig in the bloody remnants.

"It took him a while to realize that the eye on the table was not the bird's, but rather an enormous single ripped-off butterfly wing with a remarkable 'eyespot', an imitation of an eye, moving slightly from the draft, seemingly pleading for life.

Signed Knyazhna Zoryana."

"There is only one wing," said Jacob.

Jacob moved closer and inspected the body and the other wing of the butterfly that had been ground into dust and slime. He inhaled and opened his shirt to examine his shoulder. To his surprise, it did not hurt and he did not feel any damaged skin under his fingertips, only the wetness of his excessive sweat. He looked up and saw the owl sitting peacefully on Knyazhna's shoulder. Jacob whispered with collapsing sanity, "All you are, is an old angry witch! I suspect that there is nothing human in you!"

"There isn't!" Knyazhna repositioned her mouth to an endless coal mine, held it for a long while, then opened the manuscript at a specific page and began,

"There was more than a sufficient amount of humanity in me. All I had in my possession was superior human qualities. My kindness was brutally used. My beauty was butchered until it was murdered. My sincerity was salivated on forcibly by inferiors' mouths. My sacrificial loyalty was returned into my organs and bones with corroded, coarse threaded screws.

Pain is contagious, and those who were hurt are prospective offenders of others. If you are not one of them, you will be violated with the generosity of cruelty. If I could go back, I would deny all that pure human benevolence from the blood that supplied my soul and mind with mercy. I would reject my belief in good. Then, I would not end in a horridness of evil, from advancing charitable second chances.

Signed Knyazhna Zoryana."

Acknowledging that he was being given more than two chances by Knyazhna, Jacob was still making disturbing mistakes. Suddenly he was shaking like an undressed wanderer in the middle of an empty snowy field. He shivered like a kitten in a crowded place with no hope to be taken home. His mind disjointedly pulsated as would that of a researcher near understanding his failure at the collapse of theory against practice.

"Nice fur," Jacob commented on Knyazhna's wealth exhibiting outfit, trying to cross the hopelessness of the conversation into a somewhat better state, "It really suits you. Going somewhere cold? Am I going with you?"

"You have been given too many chances. However, you behaved as a common man in a common land, only reaching as far as you wanted to see at the moment, contrary to your assumption that the circumstances were orchestrated by 'the old witch'. Not that you had no ability; you did not care to make the least bit of effort. Consequently, the ordinary are bound by their lack of capacity to crossover to a higher sense, as well as a further formation of habitation," Knyazhna announced without a hint of concern.

"Maybe you are not so skilled as an instructor, Your Majesty. You could have been tutoring me in more accommodating techniques!"

Knyazhna replied sternly confronting the fact,

"Planting obstacles on the way to one's wisdom is an unneeded burden, alike the wasted responsibility of instructing the absent from the present. Those capable of tasting the ruins of the living, shall be inoculated against ignorance with incredible knowledge."

"Regardless," said Jacob and questioned pitifully, "Where do I take this lesson? What should I do with it in the end? Where do I go with that luggage of study, after I'm dead?" Then, with no desire to hear any answers, he said louder, "You know what, I remember something from your book, 'to keep you where you are.' All these morals are clearly useless brainwashing."

Knyazhna answered tiredly,

"No one knows where we should take the learned treasure of life, after it ends. Not even I. But all may see night as day. What we choose to envision is the answer. If you look long enough, you can identify anything you want. You can distinguish a deep attraction in

ugliness as well as you may uncover repugnance in beauty. Your own perception is your own world. Be indifferent or value it."

Old Knyazhna's face began to fill in with collagen inducing her skin's epidermis to look renewed and healthy. Her abdomen expanded, reversing its hollow concave. The owl took off and began silently circling around the room under the rafters. Old Knyazhna's stomach grew to the size of a late term pregnancy.

Jacob lost any connection with comprehensive judgment and willfully tried to shut his mind, "Think of nothing." He meditated with closed eyes, disengaging himself from the immediate reality.

CHAPTER 18

FINALE AWAKENING

EUROPEAN CASTLE, LIVING ROOM – LATE DAY

Absentminded of certainty, Jacob remained in a seated position at the dining table with his head resting on his crossed arms. His sleep looked as soothing as that of a deep snooze of a young puppy in a warm, loving home. By his serenity, it almost surely meant that the ordeal in his subconscious had ended.

A clock on the wall moved its spears in its usual count. The appearance of all the interior belongings were quiet normal. Outside of an open window, dried leaves and tiny particles were floating in the air, defying gravity. The sound from the outer courtyard was nothing out of the ordinary.

Slightly opening his eyelids, Jacob pulled his arms out from underneath his head. Unbeknownst to him, his previous night's horrors would be considered a baby blue shade of a child's nightmare, contrary to what would be expecting Jacob upon his awakening. Feeling the most horrific cramp in his neck muscles, followed by an inability to move, he left his head lying on the table for some time. He joked to himself, "Wait, is this my head?" He stretched his arms to either side and began to massage his neck. With a bit of a struggle, he moved the silver pot in front of his face. "Thank God it is my head," said Jacob quietly and then added, "Yeah with the weirdoes around here, you can never be sure that you won't wake up one day with a bull's head on your shoulders."

Finally, forcing himself to stand up, Jacob called out, "Yeah, okay I agree, it was not funny. I am still not sure what is going on." He shouted louder, "Hey! Good morning to you! Anybody home?! Still hiding in your night coffins? So how come I was left on the table? Aren't we like a family now? Fine, ready or not..." His stomach made a prolonged sound of hunger, "Well you are quiet boring hosts, I am ready for breakfast!"

Time took its time in bringing young Jacob's body and mind to recognize the quite different conditions of actuality. Jacob looked at the clock, which indicated twenty passed five. The weather exhibited an overcast grayness. "I guess it's the right time to wake up," he said arrogantly, "for our kind of people." After the word "people," full of good humor, Jacob covered his mouth with his fingers. There was an interesting sensation inside his rejuvenated thought. On one hand, he had 'deja-vu', the feeling as if this had happened before, but in fact it did not. In this case, the smell of emptiness was the sensation that reminded him of some other-like event. On the other hand, it was something new that he had never experienced at any time that he could remember.

For a while, Jacob searched around but located no-one. Feeling chills, he blamed the cold. Luckily, to start the fire, all he needed was right there at the fireplace. As many times before, in this oddly welcoming place, he had to wait hours for anyone to appear, so he had learned how to light the fire. Jacob reminded himself that in order to adjust to certain things in places where someone else has their own rules, he must learn to make himself comfortable, not breaking their laws relating to ethics and worship. With a distracting thought he calmed himself, "Well, we'll skip on worshiping in this house."

Hardly audible whispers resonated from the walls, "You better believe, that the house rules would be guarded as 'the Decalogue', 'The Ten Commandments from the Holy Book'." First doubting his hearing and then simply blaming the games of the cohabitants, Jacob stopped listening and concentrated on his pride of his newly obtained skill of starting a fire. The flame in the fireplace supplied the missing coziness and warmth to the room. Jacob plunged into his usual chair at the dining table, which still held cold fried pheasants, fruit and a loaf of bread. He reached for the coffee pot and even though it was cold, he poured some into his cup and drank, "God Damn it!" He spit on the floor, "It is lukewarm!" He called out with demand, "Bohdan! Bohdan! Damn it, where are you? Have you tried this coffee? It is not hot, not cold, it's lukewarm. Disgusting!"

Only while calling for Bohdan, Jacob started to sense the differences in the atmosphere and anxiety heated his chest. He pulled the white meat off a fried bird, stuffed it in his mouth and chewed silently with nervous vigor. He noticed a letter on the table and suspected, "Can it be a 'goodbye letter' without a desirable ending? I worked really hard. I was tested, insulted, abused, tried, tortured and tested again. What if old Knyazhna decides not to pay up and send me back home to LA, penniless?" Jacob's mind was throbbing as he bit down on his knuckles causing them to bleed, "What can that letter offer me? A reward or more punishment? Or will it offer anything at all?"

Confused he noticed blood, "I'm bleeding! Hey! Help!" He yelled, frenziedly hoping to hear back from his not so friendly cohabitants, "I am bleeding!" Grasping for whatever, he remembered a meditation in the form of ritual dance from one of the Middle Eastern films a girlfriend made him watch. In an attempt to recreate the meditation, Jacob began to spin in a circle with wide spread arms. Yet soon, he felt dizzy and let himself collapse on the floor screaming, "Am I suppose to bleed?!" A sudden panic came over him. He pulled himself together, returned to the table and reached for the letter.

"A single word was hand-written on the carefully sealed envelope, 'Excerptus'."

Hesitating for a few long moments, Jacob guessed at what he might have inherited, "Could it be the will for this estate, or even something more valuable?" Pronouncing 'valuable' gave him a sensation of numbness. His fidgety armpits were becoming intolerable so he opened the envelope at once. It was a handwritten single page from the manuscript. The top of the page, like all the others, was ornamented with smaller yet very elaborate writing, '*Excerptus - Child of Nosferatu.*'

He began to read hearing the strong and confident voice of Knyazhna Zoryana doubling his,

"I have reached my destination to a long lost supremacy, Youth. Gratefully to you. Therefore, I feel obligated to benefit you with certainty. You may never achieve eternal continuation. You were refuted to enter the honor of Chosen. You are not Excerptus. You will endure mortal existence, with the

unending questioning of your decisions on desires, until you learn the senseless end to all, in the absurd song of life, for dying.

Signed Knyazhna Zoryana."

Jacob lifted his body and carried his fallen spirit to the balcony for a breath of air. "Run!" screamed a voice in his head and he ran as fast as he could to the gated entrance door, the only exit from the castle. With all of his might, he forced the iron lock, trying to release the iron belted door. It would not budge. Almost immediately, Jacob came to the fact that it was secured from outside. It felt as if the iron lock and bands had fused with a wooden door. The centuries-old wood seemed to have become iron itself. Jacob turned his back and leaned against it before sliding down to the ground. There he sat for a while.

At some point, Jacob got up, and, dragging his feet, returned to the dining table. He grabbed a bottle of wine, a silver goblet, a handful of cigars and went to the balcony. Even the short distance from the corridor to the balcony reflected in his muscles, as if he had run a marathon. The idea was to catch the end of the day before he had to face the night. A night that was going to be new to him. Supporting himself on the balcony's stone rail, Jacob poured the goblet full of wine. He stood with mixed feelings; the happiness of freedom and the fear of being alone in the castle for the first time, but he was not sure it promised to be good. He lit up a cigar. Glimpsing out from the height that birds fly, Jacob noticed that his outlook on the surrounding world changed dramatically. The 'world' that was always there was now being observed and admired by him; the gray castle garden monumented with dead trees, the endless lively green land and the sunset.

Once again, Jacob unfolded the single page of the manuscript that was in the form of a letter and read word for word what he saw in front of him. As he was reading Knyazhna's voice resonated in accompaniment. He could not understand if he imagined it or it was an actual echo.

"This night will be new to you. The view will be spectacular. The green and gray land, trees of life and death, the sun that is going to meet the ground from a human point of view, painting the gloominess of dusk with red, purple and violet."

Jacob's eyes grasped and beheld the last visible range of the golden orb disappearing in the border of the ground and dust. He continued to follow Knyazhna's composition in a whisper, with the residue of self-sympathy of his helpless reasoning which ran down his cheek like rain.

"Violet is the color at the end of the visible spectrum of light. The hue

between blue and the invisible ultraviolet, the royal color of night and, invisible to others; your nightmare."

The word 'nightmare' echoed a few times, listening to it Jacob sensed a change in nature. He heard a thundering sound and felt sudden movement under his feet. He began to read out loud, as the voice of Knyazhna infused in with permanence. Two at once sounded together, two as one.

"Evident declarations of human desire and disguised violence to ourselves and towards others, are perpetual on the way in executing our chosen wish.

Signed Knyazhna Zoryana."

The single page of the manuscript moved from a random breeze. Jacob glimpsed forward and saw rapidly appearing cracks in the soil, spreading towards the castle like a web. Despair and hot flashes were rushing through his body when something uncertain yet familiar distracted his vision. There on top of the castle's rock wall stood the tender Excerptus. Emotionless like a monument, in her wind-flicked white chiffon dress that resembled a flag of surrender.

Excerptus was far away yet her voice resonated within reach,

"Look behind. You must always see the trail of the present that is gone. Was it worth the battle for living?"

Desperately, Jacob looked at Excerptus and then numbly behind.

"From his position on the balcony, he saw the living room where he first entered with the hope of earning significant means for a perfect future. That same room sheltered him from the outside thunder. The darkness of this very room welcomed and gifted him with the warmth of forgiveness and a feast worthy of kings. Here, he had opened a new acquaintance with youth. Here, he had tasted maturity at the peak of fleshly desire. In this very living room, at the other side of that table, he had met the end of living."

Recollecting all the experiences, Jacob considered every detail of this very room like a museum that carried the spirits of the precious passed. The distance from the floor to the ceiling was extensive. He looked up.

"There at the inner crown, covering every inch of the centuries-old rotten ceiling, hundreds of owl's eyes stared down at him. They goggled, devoid of judgment, without questioning his choices or producing fear that hounds forever after. They simply studied him as he studied them. The periodically blinking eyes of life's trespassing strangers stared at each other. It did not matter the difference of species. It did not matter the period of existence. What mattered was the coincidental collision at the moment of their trespassing and the collateral vital effect, in order to collect priceless crumbs of wisdom."

"Possibly," Jacob thought, "All of it, within the borders of this secluded territory, as if in a synthetic stimulator of a high tech laboratory, was created to assist in recognizing the riches of life. But what's the worth of it now, when I am standing at the frightening edge of it?"

Excerptus gestured for Jacob to jump. Jacob smiled, recalling how he followed her for a jump before from a smaller wall, when she landed light as a feather, gracefully and joyfully, but he did not. She, Excerptus, was a spirit and her soul had already given away all the weight of reality, if there was ever any.

Jacob's mind tried to make reason of the torment that compressed his chest, "Why do I feel the weight of stone, more so, all the stones from the wall, gathered on my sternum. What kind of guilt can carry a young man who did not actually kill anyone or steal from anyone? No doubt there was misunderstanding in the family or in a friendship but most likely nothing so major to question life or death. Yet from the experience of a sensitive person, the adaptation to a functional system of society is incredibly unfair. The clash between personalities resulting in a burden of disappointment and a small blame of lost delusion, may become a self-guillotine. The point is, if you have feelings, the object of anguish will find you." Astonished by his own thought he gazed at the weightlessness of Excerptus, wondering if she came to save him, end his enigma of confusion or bring him to a ordained finale.

"Look back," Excerptus repeated very plainly.

Looking back at the same dining room, Jacob did not see any eyes of owls. Instead, the overhead interior surface of the roof looked like an inside-out mushroom plantation. The stems of the mushrooms were growing from the inner ceiling with their caps facing out. The gills - the papery permanent ribs of the mushroom caps, somehow, Jacob identified as feathers around the owls' eyes.

"There were never any eyes of any nesting birds above. They were

always mushrooms, a fungus based growth that feeds on the soft wet area of all. 'Soft' like delicate souls with their ability to love, to empathize, to dream. And 'wet' as the sensitive souls that missed on gratitude for their given ability. Tormented by guilt, unable to undo what was done, they throw themselves into self-sacrifice, to a point of weeping."

Jacob was surprised by his own descriptive conclusion.

Jacob turned his attention outside again but Excerptus was gone, "Perhaps she was never there." Unnaturally calm, he continued to watch the cracks in the ground that were spreading like traps for prey of a black widow's web in an uncanny proximity of reaching the castle.

"The cycled events of life are stimulators, projected by our desires and disallowed by impediments. Are they the worst scenario, preparing us for crossing over the border of belief?" As Jacob recited, he imagined himself at the writing table in his bed chamber. The table he never used, like people who were given all kinds of opportunities but miscarried them as if they knew nothing of their use, simply because they were not prepared for the possibilities of the given prospect.

An outbreak of pitiful sensations, of not imprinting himself in the history of humankind, overwhelmed Jacob's mind. He wanted to be remembered. He nearly took off to his chamber to use his writing table for his newly found talent of thoughtful expression, that he dreamed of writing down. He made two steps forward, then a few back, "Well, there might not be any paper, I don't remember seeing any. And the ink, if there is some inside the drawer of that old table, it is probably dry. What's the use of my recorded thoughts? What is it going to change at the end of existence?"

A coarse papery texture suddenly bothered his fingers. Jacob looked at his hands and saw the same long page from Knyazhna's manuscript 'Excerptus Child of Nosferatu'. A crashing note of clarity on his intelligibility gouged him with disappointment and left a void of self-worth. He stated in a questioning tone,

"All I heard, I thought, and said, I was simply reading?"

Jacob tore the page to pieces and dropped them from the balcony. A few fragments were lifted by a warm upward wind and carried up high. Watching the words, that were falling and floating in the freedom of the open air, Jacob felt completely drained. He was sure it was not from the wine that he held in his weak hand, but from the exhaustion of an endless puzzle presented by the residents of this moldy castle. An insubstantial delicate butterfly-like touch, tickled the back of his neck and then it blew a passing-by whiff into his ear. Suspecting a breeze and the remnants of the manuscript, Jacob turned to see. There in the castle's courtyard on a broken branch of the tallest dead tree, settled the once hateful owl. They stared at each other like the few times before. For Jacob, it was an obvious omen. He had survived fourteen minutes and fourteen hours after the evil cuckooing, but was this the predicted fourteenth day, the last day of his life? He could not even guess, because he had lost track of time. There was no way of following days in the castle, except for noticing light turn into darkness and writing it down, which he never did. "It's not like they need a calendar. These soul-sucking... they, most likely count by centuries not months," Jacob half-heartedly joked. "If it is the fourteenth day of my staying here, then I still have a fifty-fifty chance to die as well as to live because I may die in fourteen weeks or even fourteen years," he cheerfully lifted his glass to the owl in a toast. The owl took off, rattling and cawing like a crow. Before disappearing from the view, it hooted twice.

A strong noise, like that of a fast train running through a tunnel, disturbed Jacob's contemplation. Knowing there was no railway near, he continued to observe the dark cracks in the ground spreading toward the castle. A low deep pitched noise, reminiscent of rocks grinding in a rupturing fault, became stronger. Suddenly a booming clash shook the walls of the castle. With one hand, Jacob grabbed onto the rail of the balcony. Similar to a ripple-effect in a rope, the seismic waves shuddered throughout his arm, deep into his core and down to his knees, releasing the centuries-old built-up stress of the Earth.

Reflecting the very end of the day, dirty blue clouds under lit with ugly fiery orange separated and, like an angel, a white swan fell from the thundering sky. The helpless bird appeared wounded. To Jacob, it resembled the fragile Excerptus with her broken wandering soul. He suddenly remembered the legend of the white swan that was silent through-out all of its life preparing the most enchanting aria for its finale. Jacob had no knowledge of the bird's musicality, nor if the gorgeous bird was actually willingly mute during its existence or if it would vocalize at death. What he saw and heard, through his new widened vision, was regrettably magnificent.

"The fall of the striking swan became a long and perfect, as possible as death could be, glide down. The divine bird was exhaling a series of tender mournful sounds that resonated at times like the soft running of musical notes in a harmonic scale, penetrating the world with its remarkable melody.

Blinded by the brightness of the light and the magnificence of death, the exquisite white swan was gracefully dying while skillfully singing its most glorious nostalgic tribute to life."

Jacob extended his arms out like a naïve child would do in hope to catch a falling star from a great distance. A bundle of powder feathers landed onto his out-stretched hands. This cloudy fluff turned into a crumbled single page. Jacob unfolded it, finding the remains of the manuscript, "Excerptus Child of Nosferatu". The voice of Excerptus filled in the words that Jacob had missed reading in his scattered haste to adapt to the world.

"Until you learn the senseless end to all in the absurdly performed, most dazzling tender song of life, for dying.

Signed Knyazhna Zoryana."

The falling heavenly bird saw her destiny through wide-open eyes, while its feathered body struck a dead tree on its way down and a spear-like branch thrust through the beating heart and under its weight, broke. Penetrated by wooden death, life hit the ground and its flesh sprinkled innocent blood.

Jacob's legs shook uncontrollably not from the soil eruptions that could take his own life, but from his empathy to the other soul that God knows what had suffered from.

Jacob hungrily grasped at the view of nature, thirstily inhaled, and lost his balance watching himself descend rapidly into the unknown.

"The weightless swan rose from the coarse ashen land and soared back to the sky where she belonged."

THE END

ABOUT THE AUTHOR

"If my life was not so tragic, I would have probably become a scientist or a creator of a comedy sitcom, because I am obsessed with details, dedicated to education, and love to laugh and enjoy making everyone around me happy. However, multiple traumas often made my life solitary, my thoughts and books were an escape from the roughness of reality." ~ YGL

Yeva-Genevieve Lavlinski grew up in Odessa, Ukraine, where she discovered her love for film, acting and art. After she graduated Art School and Law School, she moved to California to pursue her dream in American filmmaking. She currently lives in Santa Monica, California.

Yeva-Genevieve has written a number of original screenplays across multiple genres: *Excerptus: Child of Nosferatu* (basis for the novel), *Farmers Market*, *Winter Bride on a Winter Ride*, *Sand Snowman*, *Doll Hunter*, *Shoots of Spring*, *Lola Wood*, *The Night Tailor*, and *F-Listers: Of the Off-Red Carpet*. She has also written a children's book (*Good Will Doll*). Her short film *Snow Snowman* about the fall of the Soviet Union and the displacement of individual lives has won multiple awards, including Best Thriller, and was aired on TV in Europe, North America, the Middle East and North Africa for three years.

The life of this petit adventurer began in the family of a former Red Army officer Grigoriy Garbuzenko and former nurse Tamara Frunze-Sologub. A surprise child, with her older siblings, her artist sister Valentina and musician brother Anatoliy already grown up and out of the house, Yeva's early years were mostly homeschooled. Her father taught her chess and mathematics, while her mother set the example of seeing the good in all, through forgiveness and kindness as an orthodox Christian.

Little Yeva was never accepted by her

schoolmates, who were not tolerant of her progressive point of view, neither were her teachers. In fact, her third-grade professor tore up Yeva's first written composition, not believing that she wrote it.

From sixth to eighth grade, Yeva represented her new school in Odessa Regional Academic competitions, winning first place in creative writing, mathematics and physics. Yeva gives inspirational credit to her teacher, Taras Prokopechko, and Dean of Vizirka school, Nadiya Ivanivna Guchok .

By age fourteen, Yeva moved far away from home to a professional college. The following year, a tragic accident left Yeva damaged and in bed with very little hope of recovery for over eight months. Soon after and determined to stay strong, she was accepted into the Odessa Mechnikov University. That same year, Yeva had an art exhibition at Odessa's East and West Museum, which she dedicated to her beloved father, Grigoriy who was brutally killed just prior.

Not even 18 years of age, Yeva took on the responsibility of taking care of her sister, who struggled through a series of disabling car accidents, and their mother who suffered with conditional anxiety caused by their family tragedies. Love of film was a savior for Yeva, so she involved herself as an actress and artist in the theatre, Tour de Force.

Transferring to a Law Academy under Sergiy Kivalov, Yeva studied Civil and Criminal Law and began to work at the City Mayor's Office.

At the turn of the millennium, Yeva moved to the USA, to Southern California. Here, to support herself and her family, in 2004, she graduated from Orange Coast College, and became a Register Dental Assistant working in cosmetic dentistry in Newport Beach.

In 2005, Yeva was honored to become a Citizen of the United States of America. That same year, she had a sold-out Art show in Bergamot Station, Santa Monica.

Yeva's first acting debut came in 2007 from the film, Crank - High Voltage. It led to another goal of hers, joining the actors union, SAG-AFTRA, in 2008.

Being a "struggling actor," due to the entertainment industry strikes of 2009, forced her to return to work in oral surgery in Santa Monica. In 2010 she completed Graphic Design and Web Development program in the Academy of Entertainment and Technology in Santa Monica College.

A year later, Yeva studied Film Production,

Script Writing, Directing, Stage Light and Film Editing. 2013 launched Yeva-Genevieve Lavlinski's writing, directing and producing debut with her award-winning 35-min film, *Sand Snowman*.

In 2016, her life was struck with tragedy once again. Her brother was killed, which resulted in her mother having a major heart attack. All of this she held in disguise, without any obvious tears, but the horrifying wounds in her heart put her into a severe depression. Love for her mother and dedicated determination to follow her American Dream, keeps her going forward.

Her most current achievement happened in 2018, when this novel Excerptus - Child of Nosferatu is published, with the hope of many more to come.

By Paul Hamilton Molinsky

35987135R00155

Made in the USA
San Bernardino, CA
16 May 2019